Magikaspar

Stephanie Mullins Sellers

CONTENTS

ACKNOWLEDGMENTS

Thank you, Lord, for the gift of wonder and all those people you have sent my way to enrich my life as sharp stones underfoot to teach me how to be compassionate and for the empathic encounters when I was the stone.

1 ALL ABOARD

A phantasmal voice said the winner of the best class presentation received a leading role in a new teen movie about a girl escaping an island of biting dodo birds, and I anchored down atop my bed.

From the doorway, Harold told me to get out of bed for breakfast. When I didn't get up, he came in and teased me as he poked my legs and arms with a dull pencil tip.

I still didn't move. I couldn't. The apes would find me.

Harold touched my cheek, grunted, and his bare toes skidded down the hallway and back into my room with a thermometer. The cool glass slid under my tongue, and he pulled it out a minute later, his orange juice and buttered toast breath falling over me. "It's one hundred one. You have a leukemia flare, Jackie. Be still." His warm fingertip gently tapped my cheek, and he pulled off the quilt and covered me with the sheet before he fled across my thick bedside rug out my door, his toes squeaking hurriedly down the hall toward the kitchen. "Call the doctor. It's a flare." His voice drummed as a clatter filled the house with the Monday morning rush to get out the door.

"Or she's just puttin' on. Jackie ain't happy with her map." Dad's coffee cup clanked against the glass table in the dining room. "She pullin' the same junk she did with her science project last year—waited an extra day so she could take first place. I'll prove it." His voice trailed off. "Non, don't start, cher. The doc said she's in remission. We treat her like we always done. That's what she asked for." His cup clanked again. "Got a whole mess to do at da restaurant today."

"I put the thermometer in her mouth and her lamp was off, Dad."

Mom mumbled and Dad warned her, "My plate's full dis mornin'," and clapped his hands at her.

Her signature staccato knife chops thwacked her wooden cutting board. Chuck, chuck, thawk. Chuck, chuck, thwak. The skillet sizzled and Cajun seasonings broke the stale summer scents trapped in the house, humming with central air conditioning under North Carolina's blazing sun.

"Mais, listen here, ma chère. She makes herself sick worryin' 'bout gettin' dem A's. I'll tear it up right now, and you'll see. She ain't even gonna get outta bed." Mumbling and shoving sounded as their footsteps neared, Dad's clapping boots with Harold's toe taps following after.

My door creaked. Paper ripped. Slowly, at first, followed by crunching and faster ripping. Pieces grazed against the wooden floor. Dad's minty aftershave spilled over my face under his deep coffee-and-cream breaths. His hand swept across my forehead. "Tsk, tsk." And their footsteps sounded down the hallway, back into the kitchen.

"Did you see my books on her floor?" Harold's hushed voice failed his discretion efforts. "On the floor? For the Love of Lemurs on Madagascar, that's on loan from my science teacher and she'd better take care of it." Harold slapped something paper down on the counter. "She stole it from my room. And Dragonfruit is brand new. Remember, Mom? You gave it to me for my birthday. I haven't even finished it." He bit into an apple and chewed. "She'll let that dog shed all over 'em."

Mom's leather flats tapped around the kitchen, as her flavorful homemade chicken soup warmed the hallway with a mother's love and drifted into my room. Dad flushed the toilet and washed his hands in their bedroom bathroom. Harold spat brouhaha about doing my chores and did not want to walk Piper because he still hadn't taken out yesterday's trash and hated being late.

"I gotta head out early," Dad bellowed from the hallway. "Dem customers be hollerin' for my shrimp gumbo, and we goin' pick up fifty pounds o' shrimp."

"Can you walk Piper now?" Mom asked.

"It's seven-fifteen." Harold's voice went soprano like he'd scream. "I don't have time now, just put him out back. You guys don't understand. I've got more homework than her and eleventh grade is a lot more demanding than the ridiculous stuff they make seventh graders do. It takes a lot more time for everything, and you guys need to understand that. I'm getting ready to break out on my own. I'm developing a social climate around myself for college to figure out where I'm going. It takes time to decide who's in my circle, and I don't have time to do it all." Harold's tiptoes chirped across the kitchen tiled floor and stalked down the wooden hallway floor back into his bedroom and his door slammed.

"I'm gon' count to three, and you best make up your mind to get on back out here to the circle that feeds your teenage tail and do what you been told," Dad yelled after Harold and more gently, announced it was raining.

Lightning cracked and Piper fitted his one-hundred ten-pound German Shepherd frame under my bed to hide, snagging my tropical flowered quilt as he went under, and I imagined Piper on the quilt's yellow flowers in a sea of green. He formed a lump under the bend of my knees, and his head bolted upwards from the cooking commotions and its promise of scraps.

Mom's soup spoon plonked and twanged, and I saw that soup in my head turn to mush as her silence dictated she was biting her lip while the soup pot boiled and popped and its liquid churned up crashing waves.

Tink! Seconds later, the lid whistled it was our last chance to escape the beating spoon and a paprika and garlic cloud, and a roasted bell pepper and onion cloud, swirled down the hallway into my room and over my bed as tears ran down my temples. Blackness held my head still as a shimmering bright light pierced through a snagged hole in the heavy gray curtains that separated me from this world, forcing me further away.

The tectonic plates broke free from one another, and I was trapped on the Dark Continent with frantic primates of every species. Little fuzzy monkeys hung from vines, and tall, slim lemurs swung from tree limbs. While the big, heavy monkeys ambled across the forest floor as quadrupedals, their knuckles shining. It was a fight for life between the monkeys and the lemurs. They howled, hissed, growled, pulled tails, and punched stomachs. Species crossed territorial boundaries, and that meant war—blood trickling, bones bared, no-one-spared war.

My arms twitched, and my hands ached as the hair covering my caramel skin stood on end, and I imagined my ringlets tightening up from the dense humidity. I lurched up the tall palm trees, enduring deep cuts to my bare limbs to chew off the palm tree's thick fronds with my enormous canines. I jumped down into a lemur troop of about thirty furry friends and wove the fronds together. Somehow, they understood me and one by one; the lemurs followed my cue, climbed the palms, and wove the fronds together. I ordered them to ignore the hurricane-force winds and lightning strikes and showed them how the rafts worked like kicking boards, and during my fast demonstration, some of the smaller lemurs sat on top of the raft. Their long arms worked like paddles at the water's edge as heavy rains pierced through our thick fur, stinging us numb to the weather threat as the apes banged their chests after us.

"Eek-eek!" a lemur screamed as a team of apes lurched from the forest.

The apes barred their teeth and rushed the beach.

In a magnificent rush to the shore, the lemurs and I held on tight to our makeshift rafts, kicking and paddling our way to Magikaspar Island. But we didn't go far before three lost their rafts to the strong Mozambique Channel.

"Over here!" I led them to a quiet beach and sent the lower social class males into the forest for long, straight limbs. They returned in minutes with bundles of limbs, and I showed them how to weave the limbs into their rafts to make a single large raft. "We're going to make that thirty-mile trip."

"Eek-eek! That'll take days. We need food!" A male ring-tailed lemur stretched out on his hind legs.

"Quick! Strip the leaves and tender plants and fruit of any kind and push them into our raft. And you guys, you big guys, bring us four strong limbs, and we girls will get some vines," I yelled.

They wove the large limbs as a frame around the raft and jumped aboard as the king of Magikaspar made himself known.

The golden fossa peered out from under a downed kily tree's

branches. The mighty predator's eye teeth poked up its upper lip, exposing its razor incisors. Its full muzzle inched out from under the kily's cover of yellow blossoms, and the fossa dove into the cove and out to sea after us.

2 PHANTASMATIC

"Hey, Jackie," Harold howled.

I heard him. I knew it was him. I was certain. But I couldn't open my eyes. From the dark deep behind my heavy eyelids, reality collided with the mysterious.

Harold howled out from behind the family sedan's back seat as Mom dropped me off for seventh grade at Magic Kaspar School. It was a ring-tailed-lemur-only school serving elementary through the eighth grade. I only knew that because it said so in smaller letters on the sign. Harold went to the progressive inner-city school where lemurs of all species attended. They still had a few skirmishes, but school had trained their instinctive prejudices out of them during the earlier grades. The training angle had a variety of lemur species as teachers and staff, along with correlating inclusion lessons with our subjects.

I'd been questioned about my prejudice level because I was adopted into a mixed family, so everyone, teachers and students, thought I'd automatically be deprogrammed. Believe me. It is not automatic. I know because I was cursed with it, my hospital ankle bracelet tripping me up all the time because I never stopped wondering if I should hate a white or dark birth mother for walking away from me or a white or dark father. I wondered about all adults, and I think that's what made me so outspoken, as my teachers wrote in the comment section on my report cards.

The educational training program helped prevent all out territorial wars, like we read about in history. Historically, babakotos slaughtered ring-tailed lemurs that invaded their territories at night to scoop up wilting flowers from the forest floor.

When my brother teased me, he looked like a regular slaughterer. "Want your lunch?" Harold, a babakotos, also known as an indri lemur, hadn't trimmed his wild ears in forever. His yellow eyes darted at me from his hefty twenty-pound frame. He stood up in the seat, shook his musty coat, and cackled. His sour breath made my fur bristle.

My fur? When his nubby tail twitched as he danced around in a circle, I thought about how real it seemed, that it wasn't a surprise how his rank breath spewed from the back seat and landed on my tongue to the distaste of my olfactory receptors, and I screamed, "Brush your teeth!" and bounded down the sidewalk, almost like any normal morning.

Yet, nothing seemed normal in my head because I kept telling myself it couldn't be true. But I could feel it in my awkward steps, see it, smell it, taste it, breathe it, and smack; it slapped my eyes open. But the light was so bright, all I could see was stars. My mouth gapped open, and tongue pressed down between my teeth as something slid down my throat. I don't know what it was, but I knew one thing for sure; we were trapped in a phantasmatic land.

I ran back to the car, and Harold dangled my ladybug decorated lunch bag over the back seat. I reached in and tugged at the handle, and he pulled it back, clicking his teeth in a male dominant threat to eat the entire bag.

"Eek! Eek!" Aghast, I covered my mouth over my shriek.

Harold's hyena cackle stopped short as he prepared to throw something at me.

"Stop it, pups!" Mom squealed as she gripped the steering wheel. Her silky sifaka tail stiffened as her powder puff palm reached back to swat us.

When Harold dropped my lunch bag onto the back seat, I grabbed it with my free hand, popped it into my mouth, and gripped it with my teeth. I dashed away with long, sweeping steps. My essay was in a red folder in one hand and my large, colorful state map in the other. My bookbag bounced against my back as I hurried into the school and the first bell rang.

"Monday lunch is thistles, flowers, and beetle casserole," the speaker screeched.

"Hilarious." I guffawed and when I licked my lips, panic ran up my spine.

I dropped off my bulky state map in Mr. Zack Zootanna's geography classroom, who suddenly seemed much shorter. He was a fork-marked lemur with two black broad stripes over his forehead. There was a colorful jumbled pile of maps on the book counter under the window, with the thick forest view on the other side of the playground. My heart raced when the geography classroom's outside door cracked open, and I lurched forward as if I might jump out the door into the clear bright light. It was crazy. I'd never felt like jumping into the wild before. But the jungle in the distance knew my name and sang it. ┐┐┐

I imagined my birth parents somewhere safe out there, like up in a kily tree calling, "Jackie."

"Get to class. I'll see you soon. You'll do just fine, Jackie," Mr. Zootanna said. Behind him, on his desk, sat the golden trophy. A sculpted slender hand with pronounced knuckles and sharp claws gripped its finial, and I imagined it as my hand.

In the hallway, I realized something. Our teacher was a lemur too, but I wasn't alarmed, and thought he should trim the hairs under his eyeglasses because they were sticking to the glass. His long gray eyelashes stuck out over the wire rims like antennas. And somehow, all this was not alarming.

"Jackie, come here," Lilliana said. "I like your dress. I didn't realize you were a blue. It's your color."

Lilliana, a ring-tailed lemur, was my best friend. She looked cute with her black muzzle tapering into a heart-shape between her eyes. In her overall front pocket, a squirming thick caterpillar poked out its head and looked right at me.

"Thanks, Lil. What's up?" I fought the urge to snatch that caterpillar and swallow it.

I walked with Lilliana into English class. The new classroom posters featured our next semester's topic, Romeo and Juliet. Shakespeare's mouse lemurs wore formal gowns and Romeo's rags were chromatic green with black threads stitched in places where he'd torn his britches. "I can't believe the artist didn't give that poor boy a shirt. He's so scrawny," I said.

Lilliana smirked and agreed. She wrapped an arm around my shoulder and whispered. "The guys found a kily tree in the jungle less than two miles from the other side of our playground. They're going right after school today. Go with me?"

"No way. They'll be totally out of control, girl. Those old kily trees might be good for making a raft, but they also make a boy daft, my mom always says. I think. I heard it somewhere." My head was spinning, so I sat down, sweeping my tail out from the backrest. My tail? I had a tail? I jerked on it and my head tilted back and splintered down to the bottom of my spine. The realization made me feel so discombobulated that I held my tail in my lap, and that's when my hands surprised me and reassured me all the same. They were furry, gray, and wiry down to the rounded ends and my palms were black as a starless sky. They had the same number of digits, the same type of grooves, and were slick, too. I leaned back and studied my tail and took a deep breath as the classroom filled with my classmates—ring-tailed lemurs.

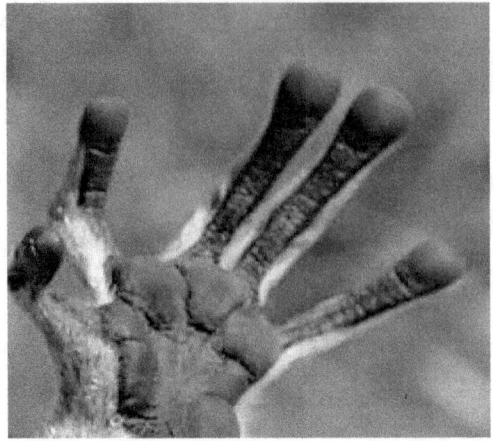

I turned to the left. Ring-tailed lemurs in jeans and tees, in khaki pants and pullovers, and in dresses and tennis shoes lurched over desks and hopped into chairs. They chattered, clacked, and shrieked on one side of the room and smaller ring-tailed lemurs yipped as they took the desks near the front of the teacher's desk. A pair of boys munched on a desk's laminate top and spit out the glued wood chips onto the floor.

I turned to the right and Ms. June Gull, a bamboo lemur, entered the classroom in blue pants and a pink blouse. A paper bag lunch clenched in her big yellow teeth swung, hitting her chest as she knuckle-walked to her humongous desk in the corner.

"Open your textbooks to page ninety-four. Read the first three pages and write the key points. Put your name at the top of the page, if you want a grade," Ms. June Gull said.

Lilliana and Shanelle, sitting on each side of me, opened their books.

While I ran my furry fingers through my tail fur. It was two feet long, with thirteen stripes of black and white, ending with a black tip. All eyes were on me. And they had their heads lowered, like I was on a tall chair or something, and that's when it first hit me. I must be the smart kid as a lemur like I was in real life, whatever that was anymore. When I sat up straighter, my tail sailed free, and it projected from over my shoulder, and my two best friends smiled at me.

"I was afraid you were sick or something," Shanelle said.

"Yeah, like who would lead us if you got sick or something?" Lilliana asked.

"No screeching!" Ms. Gull said.

Horrified, I closed my mouth.

English class ended with only three boys sent to the office for leaping and stink fighting. They were the new boys, the ones from the other side of Magikaspar's southern forest. Brock, Kane, and Rowdy had been banned from the best habitat area in the southwestern habitat for selling kily tree wine for the second time. Everyone drinks kily wine, but we water it down to dilute the alcohol, so it's like a fruit juice. It's made with rainwater, and we add fruit because the containers most of us use for collection can have funky aftertastes.

We collect rain in any container we can roll home. My family had a collection of salad containers hidden in a rusty metal bird cage on the back deck. They are glass, so they are difficult for a stranger to see, and they don't have an aftertaste most of the time. The coleslaw containers hold a sulfur taste, but Mom rinses them with vinegar to remove it. She's so smart. The containers are about one gallon each, and we ration the water. We take showers outdoors, like most families, when it rains. Other times, we use a damp cloth or Mom just spits on her hands and preens us all over and she gets to drink the cup of water. Mom is the water keeper, like all the other moms.

The water shortage on the island is dire. Our elders are dying from dehydration and poisoned water. And it's all because of the nickel mine, the biggest in the whole wide world. Anyway, we talk about water a lot because there's not enough, and kily tree's tamarind fruit wine is a household necessity.

The problem with the boys' wine was that it was full strength liquor and only the bad boys drank their tamarind fruit "wine". I say that because the alcohol makes them bad. The newspaper said they'd hiked to town and pooled their coins to hire a cousin to drive them to Lake Tsimanampetsotsa. They filled jugs with the lake's salty water, so salty no fish live there, and sold it to tourists when they arrived at the national park. With their profits, they bought Campden tablets to kill bacteria and glass bottles, stole copper pipes from a plumbing supply shop, and with two old coffee percolators, and over the course of four weeks, they kept a fire going and made liquor and called it wine. What they didn't drink they sold to tourists. At least they showed initiative.

They had to spend a long time, like a week, on their own in the jungle as their punishment. After their survival tenure, all alone in the jungle, they were allowed to attend school on probationary status. Everybody knew about those boys.

Lilliana and Shanelle followed Jackie into geography class and took their seats. While the boys raided the pencil sharpener for lead and pencil shavings. They spread the silver lead over their white faces, making mustaches and clapping for one another. When Mr. Zootanna entered the room, Brock ate the evidence in his hands, but Kane and Rowdy sprinkled their shavings behind their backs.

"Do you need another discussion with the headmaster, boys, or should I say, sirs? I can get you an immediate appointment with those striking mustaches." He sat a stack of International Geography magazines on his desk and turned around to look at them again and howled rounds of laughter. "Sirs, please, sit down. Right now." Fork-marked lemurs were big talkers to make up for their small size, and Mr. Zootana was true to his species. He made me jump in my seat.

The second bell rang, and I pulled out my state essay on Mississippi from the red folder. Ready for that trophy and tickets to summer camp. There were fourteen students and eight were girls. We sat on the opposite side of the class and watched the boys squirm and stink fight behind the teacher's back.

"Do you recall the self-control policy? It is in effect. Disturb the presentations today and you earn twenty points off your grade. No talking, no honking your nose, no laughing, no nothing." Mr. Zootanna pushed the podium toward the center of the open area in front of the desks. His bald spot shined under the classroom's center light from where he stood behind the podium. And a row of boys smiled as their hums for social approval radiated.

"Are you going to stand there during our presentations?" Brock asked the squinting teacher as the bright sun x-rayed his recessing hairline.

"No, the presenters will. Why?"

"The glare." Brock squinted; his hand cupped over his brow.

"Jackie, do you mind if Brock gives his presentation first?" Mr. Zootanna winked at me.

"No, sir." My tail flicked in Brock's direction.

"Stupid," Brock mouthed.

"Minus five and counting." Mr. Zootanna hummed.

Brock pulled a wrinkled paper from his notebook and made his way to the podium in a quadrupedal form, dragging the paper across the floor.

"Have somebody hold up your state map," Mr. Zootanna said.

"Kane," Brock said, and pointed to the map pile. "It's the red one on Louisiana, the party state—New Orleans." His lips rounded over his long canines as he prepared to howl, and the teacher stopped him.

"Eek-eek!" Mr. Zootanna's long arm warned.

Brock's tail was missing chunks of fur, and food stained his white belly, but his jeans were clean.

"Pull your shirt down. We don't want to see what you ate for breakfast," Mr. Zootanna said.

Brock looked down at his round belly and grinned. "That was dinner last night." He pointed to a yellow-orange stain and then to a red stain. "That was breakfast." He pulled down his shirt and raised his chin to his boy troop on the far side of the room.

"Louisiana is famous because New Orleans is the festival capital of the world. But its state capital is Baton Rouge. It has festivals for all kinds of food, like crayfish, those big crawdads you can catch in a creek, and music, and for all kinds of races, and being Greek, and tacos, tomatoes, and wine!" Brock pointed to the wine bottle on his map. "But the most popular festival is Mardi Gras." Brock jumped so high he tapped the ceiling tile. "I want to get my troop up there one week when we get our licenses."

Desks rumbled and chairs rocked as students fought barreling laughter. Mr. Zootanna held his hand over his mouth and his cheeks burned red.

"What?" Brock asked. His lips hung out over his bristly chin.

Mr. Zootanna contained himself and told Brock to continue. "Tell us about the demographics and levee issues."

"The what?"

"Surely you included the levee catastrophes."

"Yeah, yeah, yeah, the levees on Lake Pontchartrain. I like that name," Brock said. "My mom said to write that sentence in here. Let me find it now." His hand ran the length of the paper. "I think it's on the other page." He lurched on his two hind legs back to his desk and grabbed a paper from his notebook. "Yeah, this is it. Mom said humans will do anything for a dollar, even build houses where water lives. Idiots." At the podium, he tried out a serious look on his boys in the far corner. "Lake Pontchartrain leaked into homes and roads and made a disaster area in 2005 when the winds forced the water out of the lake. For a while, people blamed the broken levee on the new levees built in upper-class neighborhoods because most of the damage was in the older poor neighborhoods. But hurricanes aren't prejudiced like that, and neither is the wind. Sometimes, a fella just gets caught up in a storm and has to make the best of things. Might be why they have all that wine over there."

A slight smile formed on Mr. Zootanna's muzzle. He nodded and

Brock shared statistics he'd found on the school computer.

"One of the most interesting things I learned is that Louisiana is a wet place to live and if there's ever a global drought, we ought'a think about getting there, for water." Brock nodded for Kane to put the map back in the pile, and the class clapped.

"Good critical thinking skills, Brock. Good job," Mr. Zootanna said. "Jackie, you're next."

Lilliana followed me to the front of the classroom, fetched my map on Mississippi from the pile, and stood next to me. Lilliana was a few inches shorter, but on her hind legs, all stretched out and in sneakers, it was hard to tell how many inches. Besides, Lilliana's mom stroked her daughter's top head out with saliva on her front comb teeth, so her hair stood straight up, giving her another inch. I stretched my neck upward, and my red eyes darted at Lilliana.

"Mississippi is the Magnolia State, and its capital is Jackson. It has many native residents, but they were forced to move from their homeland to a different land in the state. It made me think about how we lemurs were bullied, well, we fled for our lives, from our home in Africa. But most of us like Magikaspar, and I think the natives in Mississippi should do like us and just get over it and do like Brock said; make the best of it.

The name of the state was given by a group of natives who were traveling through and didn't even call the land their homelands. Which is another thing about Africa. It got its name from a traveler too, Leo Africanus, who was just writing about everything he saw. And Magikaspar got its name from a traveler who did not even step on the island. He was just another writer-traveler, Marco Polo, and researchers think he read the map wrong, and our island was stuck with it. This is an example of people influencing geography, like forever. Anyway, I want to influence everybody now and get our island's name changed to something respectable, by people, um, by primates who live here. I like Lemur Land. We might begin a revolution and declare it is time, in 2025, to update geographical titles to reflect the current trends. We are on the fourth largest island on Earth, and you'd imagine some other islands and countries will even get the hint and make a name for themselves, too. If we listen to stats, and if we can get other species to listen to female leaders, they'd understand the logic, like in Mississippi's stats.

There are a ton of statistics about Mississippi, and the ones I thought about most were that it is 51% female, with a population of only 23% college graduates. Females live longer, make more people, um, or in our case lemurs, so they need more schools. They need hospitals more than males and need more funds, overall. College graduates buy more property, invest in communities, volunteer more, and donate more, and make up more of the elected officials in the communities. That means that some of Mississippi's females, especially the elderly who need a room in a nursing home, are underserved, are suffering or risk death because they can't get help. It takes a lot of money to care for the elderly. I have a solution for that, too.

Make females the leaders in all community organizations when there are not enough college educated citizens to contribute to a healthy property tax rate. Women know it's a waste of money to plant flowers on the highways, and we do not need to send ten males out to pick up trash off the highway, when it only takes three, if they don't stink fight all day long.

And it's a waste of money to hire planners when commissioners should just have a female draw out a city plan. We multi-task by instinct." (Mr. Zootana's lips hung, exposing his shiny teeth and curled tongue below his bulging eyes.) "Females hunt, plan homes, and care for the elderly, and their babies. Males only hunt and stink fight. We need to use the males for the benefit of the community. Send them to nursing schools, cooking schools, and train them to be useful to others, like females are. If it were up to me, I wouldn't even allow males to run for elected positions."

The females raved, clapped, and bounced in their seats, and the males hissed and snarled.

Kane stood up in his seat. "Those old women are sucking up all our money!"

Mr. Zootanna spat his drink across his desk with a guffaw.

"You don't know nothing. I know your brother and he said so. You don't know nothing," Rowdy burst out. He rubbed his tail over the antebrachial glands on his wrist spurs and waved them through the air.

I wondered if my brother knew something about my birth parents.

"Oh no, you don't. We're not having another stink fight in my classroom!" Mr. Zootanna pointed to the side door. "Get! Right now."

The males joined in the stink fight, some scraping their tails over their shoulder glands, smearing the brown odoriferous stink on their tails, except Neo. His rigid and bulky-boned frame held his half tail. For years, the boys tried to squeeze the story from Neo, but he rarely answered any of their questions on a regular day.

"All you boys—out!" Mr. Zootanna yelled.

The boys launched over desks, waving their tails at the girls on their way out the door. The door closed, and I asked to use the bathroom.

When I returned, Lilliana was holding the map for the red-backed ring-tailed lemur, Danita. I waited at the door, peering through the window, so I wouldn't disturb her presentation. Danita pointed at her puff-paint decorated map of Rhode Island.

"This exotic state in North America is a blend of the old world meets new world because tourism is one of the main industries," Danita said. "People come from everywhere to eat bugs like we do. Only their bugs are the sea bugs that eat junk from the bottom of the sea, and they are called lobsters. Some of their bugs weigh ten pounds!"

She had an interesting speech, but the stink fight outside the hallway's double doors out on the inner playground was more interesting.

Fingertips spread my eyes open to a blinding overhead light and white walls and white everything. Wires or something like it, thin and foreign, brushed against my chest and arms. Antiseptic hung in the air, and no one had a full face, and they all wore the same green outfits with odd caps. They called out numbers and said something about plasma, bone marrow, and being on time. Beeping and ringing and soft shoe patter swirled around me. My eyelids were set free and clamped shut, and I tried to wake up. I wanted to wake up in my own room. But heavy blankets held me down as a strange wind passed over my face and swinging doors folded shut behind me.

"Yip, yip, yip!" The boys had removed their shirts and were in a full-blown stink fight, covered in brown smears. Their cackles and twitters swept through the doors' cracks. They jumped over one another, wrestling to the ground, and grass stains streaked across their backs. They shrieked and howled, and the headmaster lurched toward them and, with his arms up over his head, roared. He was an exceptional babakoto lemur at four feet tall.

"Sit!" Mr. Intensity's bark exploded.

The boys sat, and he paced back and forth in front of them, stopping occasionally to point and snarl. It was late May, nearing ten o'clock, and the sun beamed on the inner playground area. The boys sat on their haunches, with spread legs, absorbing the warm sun shining on their bare bellies.

Through the classroom window, I watched Danita walk back to her desk, and I took one last look out the double doors. The boys were single file in a submissive quadrupedal walk toward the parking lot. It looked like they were sent home for the day.

I returned to my desk as Catrina took the podium, and Lucella held her map of Oregon for her. She had an okay presentation, but her map was the bomb. It was on a black background and had neon letters and the rivers shined with glitter. She pointed out the small park on Oregon's map. "They named a town named Idiotville because it was so remote only an idiot would live there. Then they named the creek Idiot Creek, and so on, until it was popular to be in Idiotville. And I put this headstone on it with 'Suicide' because anywhere in Oregon a person can commit suicide, and they say it was made legal to help humans with diseases die faster."

We clapped and Mr. Zootanna asked Catrina if she had any elders who were sick or in pain.

"No. My last grandmother lives with us and is still the leader. She has a knee that slows her down, but we would be real idiots to tell her to commit suicide."

"Idiots? What about when she gets down in the bed or she begs to die?" His palm cupped his chin.

"I don't know. I don't want to think about it," Catrina said.

I raised my hand, and Mr. Zootanna's chin popped free. "I think suicide for humans is different." My tail jerked upright. "Because there's so many of them and there's not a lot of us left. Each life is more precious that way. Besides, if we had lemurs choosing suicide for others, like signing the papers to have a grandmother's life cut short, there would be lawyers waiting graveside. Just think of the social inclinations. I mean, what female does not want to be the leader? I've seen females do some mean things to be leader."

"You're a leader, Jackie. Did you do something mean to get that status?" Mr. Zootanna asked.

"I don't think so. I think I'm just the leader because of my grades. I'm not sure, because..." I didn't want to say it out loud because it made it all so real. "Because I'm adopted and live in a mixed family, and I think I was a human in another life."

Mr. Zootanna blinked. "Do you now?"

Eyes opened wide and jaws dropped as the girls yipped and cackled. Even my girls, Shanelle and Lilliana, yipped. I sunk into my chair.

"Maybe you had an experience once, like a reincarnation thing. But I don't believe any living thing can shape shift or change its DNA. It all goes back to the bones. We'll talk later, Jackie," Mr. Zootanna said.

Prudence began her presentation with her map on California and recited her essay from memory. She had everyone's attention, and I was so relieved. But I thought I was the only one who was capable of memorizing that much material. Her ears were trimmed too, like I keep mine, in a straight line instead of following the curve of my ears. It seemed like she was mocking me, but I kind of liked it.

After class, I asked Prudence to sit with Shanelle and Lilliana, and me for lunch.

"Do you want to make friends with just me, or my girls, too? I can't leave them guessing, you know." Prudence's tail rose above the back of her head and pointed at me.

Shanelle jabbed my side, and my smirk grew into a gleaming grin. "We should all sit together. There's that picnic table on the playground and it's so sunny. We can warm ourselves afterward."

Prudence looked over her shoulder at Catrina and Danita as Lucella approached. She stood at Prudence's side with her feet squared up and shoulders reared back. Without looking at her troop, Prudence agreed to lunch with us.

Lucella always stood next to Prudence, like she was measuring her up, testing her, or testing her own allegiance. I felt like I could win over all of Prudence's friends if I could win Lucella.

History class filled with hums as we stole peeks at one another's repose in anticipation of the first disruption. Lucella led the sniffling, followed by every other girl coughing, sneezing, or sniffling. Our teacher stopped them when Shanelle blew her nose, and it honked dry.

"Okay, I know what's going on here," Mr. Timetails, a hairy-eared dwarf lemur, said. "That's enough." He wiggled his ears, like always, when he was excited, and stomped one stilt. He'd used stilts so students would recognize him as a teacher and not one of the groundskeepers, who were his troop members. They were from a rainforest on the eastern edge of the island.

Besides, adult ring-tailed lemurs did not make good teachers because they wanted to teach like they lived, with only females as leaders. They didn't want any males in the same classrooms.

Mr. Timetails said something about homework and had Lucella hand out rubrics. He was a beast about homework. "It's due on Thursday. No excuses."

It was only Monday, but I couldn't think about homework. I couldn't think straight at all. All I could think about was power. I could not lose my power to Prudence. I had to assert my leadership role somehow. There was no way I'd give my girls up to Prudence. And the boys, they were under me too. I had to come up with something clever, big, and something that would knock Prudence out of the boat.

One of the rubber floor protectors on Mr. Timetails' stilts crumbled into bits as he paced at the front of the class. It left a pink trail as tiny as our teacher's pink fingertips. He raised a long, thin finger at us. "You have three nights. I want you to trace the human history of when they first migrated from Mesopotamia in the ancient Middle East, to Israel, to North American, in that order. I want a paragraph in your own words explaining how and why they fled one place for another. Use your Good Book for reference and write the page numbers in parentheses."

History class was almost over, and I still didn't have a clue about how to stop her takeover. I had to pee again. I was so nervous.

As soon as the bell rang, I went to the bathroom and so did all the girls. Prudence took the first stall, and I took the last.

"Did you bring a dessert today, Jackie?" Prudence called out.

"Yes. My entire lunch is a dessert. Mom makes it special, just for me, because no one else in my family likes it." I lied.

"Oh-h."

My lunch bag was on the counter in homeroom. If I hurried, I could grab it and eat my bologna and cheese sandwich before I was found out. I rushed out of the stall, ran water over my hands, and sprang down the hallway. Super. I was the first one there. I opened my bag and the girls behind me clucked. I pushed the sandwich into my mouth and bit down.

Something strange and leathery and slimy and cold oozed between my tongue and teeth. I halfway faked a cough as I fought vomiting and turned my back to the girls who had rushed in behind me.

"I wasn't going to make you share it, Jackie. You are determined. I'll give you that." Prudence clasped her lunch bag to her chest as she ambled toward the door. "We'll be at the picnic table, if you still want to us to join you."

"We'll be right there." I tried to smile at Shanelle and Lilliana. "I have something in my teeth." I turned my back to the girls and opened my hand to reveal a clay and frog sandwich wrapped in kily leaves. My stomach heaved, and the girls asked if I needed help.

Lilliana faced me. "Are you saving that for the picnic?" She stared at my sandwich.

"Yeah."

"I just love those frog sandwiches your mom makes. Can I have a bite?" Shanelle asked.

"Sure. You know, I think I ate that nectar power bar too fast and I'm not that hungry. You want this?" I held out the sandwich, my stomach growling.

"No. Just a bite. Mom packed a mouse rolled in crushed almonds, leftovers," Shanelle said.

"This will be the best picnic!" Lilliana squealed. "I have a knife to cut up my rhinoceros chameleon and grapefruit salad. We can make a platter out of my map. It's cardboard."

"Yeah." I hurried down the hallway to the back door, planning my chatter because my belly roller coastered over the menu, and I thought I'd hurl.

3 LUNCH OF CHAMPIONS

Prudence's tail rose above her head as we approached the picnic table. She and her friends wore matching colors each day, and today was orange. Her dress had puffy sleeves, Danita's was plain with a white collar, and Lucella's had large yellow dots.

Shanelle, Lilliana, and I sat across from them. I wore blue, and Shanelle was in a pink skirt and white blouse, and Lilliana wore her signature overalls with a white tee shirt. Shanelle and Lilliana prepared the platter as I organized the napkins for us and offered them to Prudence and her girls.

"We have our napkins in our laps. Don't we girls?" Prudence said.

"Try the frog and clay sandwich. I don't know what Jackie's mom adds to hers, but they're the best. I always ask for one when I'm at her house," Lilliana said.

Bird toes stuck out from Prudence's lips, and she pushed them in with her napkin-covered finger. Danita scooped a gelled worm concoction onto a lily blossom and shoved it into her open mouth. And Lucella unzipped her bright lunch bag and a zebra dove's head popped out. "Coo. Coo," the little bird called as it lifted its wings into the air. Lucella sprang onto the table, jumping all over the place, her tail smacking us in the face and her hand smacking the dove unbalanced, and it landed in the grass. She leaped down, and the bird took flight—straight up free. In her plight to catch her dove, Lucella had stomped our lunch platter flat with black dirt and sand and whatever else Lucella infested it with from her soiled shoes.

I stealthily patted Shanelle's back, and she must've signaled Lilliana because my girls did not respond to the disaster.

Lucella returned to the table full of apologies, saying she was starving.

I knew then that Lucella was my equal. She was a fighter but balanced with heartfelt apologies. Sometimes, at least in my experience, like when I'd been caught using my brother's iPad, retribution was everything. I had to clean his room for a week and make a log of everything I borrowed from then on. Guilt held my repose as I recalled my, er, his book on Madagascar and that I hadn't written down the borrow but had snuck into his room and stolen it. Maybe today was a bad dream and was a punishment sent by the gods. The words lofted in the distance, "Do not forget to write this in the log." I wondered what would happen if I stole-borrowed Harold's Holocaust book and the images brought me back to reality; the orange-clothed girls vying for leadership.

"We have dessert, as usual. I brought my mother's baobab and jackfruit salad. There's cream on the side." Prudence opened the plastic containers and handed sharpened sticks to her girls. They broke them into halves and handed one to each of us. "We'll have to take turns sipping the cream."

My girls and I stared at the bowl of cream. It was a rare treat as there were few cattle on Magikaspar and only the wealthy had their own milk cows. We thanked her and jabbed at the smaller chunks of fruit while her girls nabbed the larger chunks. Her girls pulled the bowl of cream to their lips, exposing their dental hygiene as lacking, at best.

"Your girls don't have anything contagious; I suppose?" Prudence held up the cream in our faces.

Shanelle said milk gave her the runs.

"Me too," Lilliana said. "That's why we don't keep it at our house."

"Is that a hair?" I asked about the black hair swimming in the white cream. "Was this properly screened?" I didn't want to give the same excuses, but it was considered rude to refuse any gifts in our culture, and that hair was screaming at me, "Cow teat germs." I pushed it back from my face and told Prudence, "That could be a cat hair. Barn cats are infected with parasites."

"Oh, of course. We keep the veterinarian on call. Our cats even have their own beds, not like racoonish cats you see in other barns. Our barn cats are fed and wormed and have shots, just like our hired help. When you deal with consumables, you can't be too careful, you know. Our male lemurs, every species, has routine veterinarian care. They keep our milk cow washed and handle all the farm duties, and we trust them. Or we'd cut off one of their hands and make them wear it around their necks until it rotted. And just so you know, what you're missing; our Angus cows are shipped in from North America." Prudence poked out her tongue until it was a wiry pink limb delving into the cream. She pulled the hair off the tip of her tongue and held the bowl right in my face. "Have some. I know you want it. I don't have anything contagious. My family is purebred, you know, a full family of ringtails."

Shanelle's and Lilliana's clasped hands resting on the picnic table unclasped and matched mine as I stood. They were spread eagle.

"We enjoyed the, uh, activities today. Learned so much and we appreciate being included." I pointed to the banana trees at the edge of the school's property line, my chest heaving. "We have about ten minutes to eat any banana weevils we can find. Want to join us, Lucella? I know you're hungry."

Lucella pounced at the chance for food, her yellow dotted orange dress hopped in delight toward the banana trees. We followed after her in a jovial romp, calling out the open invitation for all who could hear. "Lunch is served! Weevil, weevil, here we come. Look out now, you'll be our gum. Over the canines and into the cavern. Weevil, weevil, welcome to the tavern!" We sang out the old men's whiskey rhyme with high hopes of finding a swarm.

"I should've followed you before," Lucella said with a mouthful of squirming black bugs. "I was starving today. I skipped breakfast because I didn't finish my homework until this morning." When she laughed, a live weevil escaped her lips, and she jumped down to her hands and knees and grabbed the booger. She swallowed him whole and asked Lilliana to please take some back to their last class of the day for her friends. "They love these."

Lilliana succumbed to a fistful of the extremely large weevils in her front overall pocket and clasped the button down tight.

Lucella waved to Prudence and her two girls at the picnic table as we passed through the rear door. "I got ya something. Come on!"

They lingered at the picnic table until the first bell rang and made it to music class as the second bell rang. The banished boys hadn't returned, and we girls were asked to play our flutes.

"What song?" Danita asked.

When there was no instant answer, we flipped to the last song we'd practiced and warmed up, blowing the chorus.

"Lilliana, come front center, dear," Mrs. Mournful, a wee mouse lemur who rode a battery-powered trike through the school, said. Her big black and orange-red eyes, pools reflecting our souls, threatened to sing our deepest secrets, since the boys were out. Everything she said sounded like a song. "Lilliana, my dear, you will bring unity to our troop at this school."

"What?" Prudence grimaced.

Lilliana's tail dragged behind her, ears flapping against the back of her head. Her stride was erect and tall, so confident. It was like her overalls had transformed into a suit and tails and she was going to conduct us or something.

"I want you to sing," Mrs. Mournful halfway whispered to Lilliana, "our French song, like we practiced, like you will sing on Friday night at graduation."

Gasps and clucks filled the room.

The white board held the title of the ancient French love song we'd practiced on our flutes. "Le Promenoir de deux amants" by Tristan l'Hemite translates to English as "The Walk of the Two Lovers," was written in 1910 and is in the public domain. Magikaspar was taken by force by the French in the mid-1800s and fell under her rule in 1896. Some believe this song is about the French invasion and the soul of Magikaspar, hungering still today for its homelands." Under this was a request for a volunteer to introduce our solo artist at out graduation's event.

Mrs. Mournful strummed the mandolin and on the second chorus of Le Promenoir de deux amants, Lilliana's strong soprano sang out and we wept in delight.

"Listen to me, dear Clémentine. Listen." Lilliana filled the room with the most longing reverberations ever heard.

Goosebumps raised the hairs on my head as visions of my birth parents on a raft down a slow-moving bayou sang the precious lullaby to me in a cradle between them.

We held our flutes hard against our hearts to keep it from escaping. We couldn't take our eyes off Lilliana. Her mournful soprano poured over us in heaping doses. Her eyes half-shut, with glimmers of light shining through. Her arms spread upward as the lyrics confessed God's gift to her.

The Walk of the Two Lovers
Near this dark cave
Where the air is so sweet
The waves struggle with the pebbles,
And light fights the shadows.

Listen to me, dear Clémentine. Listen.

Do you wish, by a sweet privilege,
To set me higher than the humans?
Make me drink from the palms of your hands,
If water does not melt the snow.
Listen to me, dear Clémentine. Listen.

My Lilliana would sing a solo at graduation, my Lilliana.

Mrs. Mournful rode over to Lilliana and reached for her shoulders and squeezed her so tightly there was no air between them. Lilliana was all smiles and so humble she could not look at us. But her eyes jumped open wide when Mrs. Mournful scratched at the top of her little head and a fat weevil slipped down her blouse into the cleavage valley.

"Oh! Oh!" Mrs. Mournful shook her blouse and squealed.

"I'll get it!" Lilliana's long fingers went down the teacher's blouse and fished around, her eyes shut tight. "I'm not looking. I promise."

"Just get that thing out! Where did it come from?" Mrs. Mournful jumped up and down.

Lilliana took it as a sign for action. She picked her up and shook our teacher upside down by her tiny feet. The weevil fell out, scurried across the classroom floor, and Shanelle grabbed it and popped it into her mouth.

"I got him, Mrs. Mournful. I got him." Shanelle shouted with her mouth full.

Prudence and her girls pointed at Lilliana. Her back was to us as she sat Mrs. Mournful back on her scooter, and the weevils roamed in all directions over Lilliana's overalls.

"Outside! I don't do live weevils. My dear Harry smashes them dead for me and peels them." Mrs. Mournful's soprano squeaked as Mr. Intensity breached the classroom.

"What's going on in here?" Mr. Intensity's expression said he saw what was happening. He helped pick off the weevils, eating the ones he caught.

"Is that all of them?" Prudence called out.

Lilliana looked into her overall pocket. "That's it. We can get more after school, if you want."

"Oh, no, no, no, I don't want..." Mrs. Mournful squealed. "Class dismissed."

"But class isn't over for twenty more minutes," Mr. Intensity told her.

She pointed down to the scooter's base and there sat her white bloomers and a sock with her shoes.

"Class dismissed," Mr. Intensity announced. "Everyone out." He led us to the door and closed it, but Lucella blocked its closing.

"I need to ask her something," Lucella told him.

"Make it quick."

"Mrs. Mournful, the boys were practicing something for graduation, too. What are they going to perform?" Lucella asked.

"I Like to Move It Move It," Mrs. Mournful blew.

"Haw!" Lucella and Mr. Intensity guffawed.

"Perfect for those impish boys," Lucella said. "I can't wait for graduation night."

"Those boys need more than a strong title to get them through my class. Seventh grade is the make 'em or bust 'em grade. And those boys are going to bust me if they don't get through puberty's rowdy stage and calm down. I'm seriously concerned. They've been seen coming out of the jungle and we all know that fossae are a beast without diet restrictions. That cat'd eat a ring-tail same as he'd eat a wild pig. In fact, he prefers ring-tailed lemurs." Mrs. Mournful looked out the window, past the mowed lawn, to the jungle's edge. "There'd be nothing left of those boys but the bones."

4 THE MAGIKASPAR NIGHTMARE

Prudence joined us under the banana trees, and her girls, Danita and Catrina carried three bottles of water and handed one to Prudence.

"Bananas are ninety-percent water," Shanelle told me. "How many should I pick?"

"We aren't allowed to climb trees on campus. It's a rule," Catrina spat.

Shanelle sprang onto the tree and was halfway up when she looked down at Catrina. (Shanelle's dad was a bus driver, and she knew there was no chance of a single adult around for another fifteen minutes. Because they were either in class or checking off their bus inspection lists before the drive home.) Her face filled, cheeks growing wide, and I told her to conserve her body's resources, and she got the message. She did not spit.

"Yer girl scaled that tree," Prudence said.

Shanelle stopped climbing, and I pointed up. She worked off a bunch of bananas and let them fall. Some burst across the grass and I told Danita to leave them on the grass and tomorrow we'd have lots of weevils. "Go ahead. Eat the fresh ones."

We each had a banana when a skirmish sounded from the jungle. Rowdy appeared, shaken and sweaty. He sprinted up to us and held his knees, catching his breath. "We need help. We won't make the bus, and we can't stay in there all night because of the fossae."

"We'll help. What do you need?" I asked. "Do you want us to call your parents?"

"No. No. Don't call anyone. We want one of you, no, two at least, to help carry a stretcher," Rowdy said.

"A stretcher?" I asked as I signaled for all of us to follow.

We were a football field deep into the jungle when the bell rang in the distance, but we had to keep going. The boys needed us. Danita stayed behind to tell Mr. Intensity where we were and for our parents to wait and to call emergency services.

Danita was a D student, and I'd questioned Prudence about her choice, but she said Danita would follow directions.

"What was that?" Lilliana stopped running and gave us the hush signal.

A hound yipped, followed by the boy's screeching.

Geesh, I thought, if the hounds are attacking that's one thing, but if they're still in hunt mode, you'd think those boys would keep quiet and hide.

"Come on. We're almost there!" Rowdy led the way.

The boys were at the kily tree, about two miles from the school. I was sure because my track time was 6:20, and the sun was at a quarter past three. Considering the bush interference and vines, and such, we'd made good time.

Neo didn't even look up at me. His molars ripped bark into shreds, and he wove it through opposing strips as Kane and the other boys held the loose stretcher, taking shape. Brock laid on the stretcher, moaning and holding his arms clasped over his bare chest and the white shin bone's jagged edge burst above the crimson meat next to the failing tourniquet.

"Anyone a girl scout?" I checked their curious reflections as Lucella stepped up.

"Just cry, Brock," Lucella said. "My mom tells me to cry when I get hurt, and it works. It lets some of the pain out." She stroked his head with her fingertips. "I'm going to check your pulse and then we're going to tighten the tourniquet."

"No," Brock cried. "It's killing me."

"You'll bleed out." Lucella splashed the bloody pool with a stick. "See? If we don't fix it, it will kill you."

"Lucella? Are you serious? Where'd you learn this?" Prudence asked.

"My parents are doctors. Suddenly forget that? Duh?" Lucella rolled her eyes, picked up a stick, tested its tooth, and wound it around the seeping red shirt's tufted knot. "This is going to help, but it will hurt, Brock," she told him.

He groaned. Not an ordinary groan, but the kind that you feel deep in your guts, like a punch. The boys looked away, and we girls didn't.

"Help me strip this bark," I told Shanelle and saw Lilliana at the kily tree's trunk base, leaning over. "What are you doing?"

"An elder." Lilliana stood. "He's not doing too good. He looks like a prune, all dried up."

"We can fix that, too. You strip bark and take it to Neo," I told Shanelle, and pounced over to Lilliana. "He can suck the sap out."

The old ring-tailed lemur, curled up in the fetal position, slowly offered his quivering hand. Lilliana took his hand, stroking the back of it, and told him to be still. "We're going to help you get out of here."

"This is my home, child." His weak words pulled us closer. "I would like to get up on that limb though before you leave. Hurry. Hurry before they get here."

The limb he pointed to was a good ten feet up. I bit my bottom lip and asked the elder if he was strong enough to hold on to Rowdy's back. "I'll have him get you up there and stay with you until you are okay. He can bring you food while you regain your strength."

"That is too much." He closed his eyes, sucking the sap from the tree bark.

Lilliana's worried expression flashed when the old man sucked the bark dry. He said he wanted more.

"Would you collect some water, Lil? Check the bamboo leaves. There's always some in the base of the leaves." I pointed to a bamboo outcrop, and she asked what to put the water in, and I told her to use a bamboo section. "Hasn't your mother taught you how to collect water from bamboo?"

"We don't go into the jungle. She worries about the hunters. I fetch water from the house gutter." Lilliana looked over her shoulder at me. "Hey, your mom is a sifka. They don't drink water. Why would she teach you how to find it?"

"Because she's the leader, and it's her job. Now get that water," I yelled, then mumbled, "Does Lil think we don't wash our dishes and clothes? Geesh." I asked the elder, "What's your name?"

After some hesitation and his struggle to rise onto his haunches, "Doron."

With my eyes held in his, I shouted to Lilliana that we needed water for Brock, too.

"What are you doing, living here?" I asked Doron.

"Gang wars are not for old men."

"But you were a great fighter. We all know about your deeds and cleverness. Abrikita must be mad or just plain evil to send you away." I held his hand.

"We lost touch after her mother and I talked her into giving up her daughter for adoption. She was not old enough to parent, and we were just too old."

My head swirled, whirlpooling with phantasmic ideas as I stared into his intrepid eyes, wondering, hoping, I'd found the connection. "How can anyone do that, send someone away?"

His lips parted in a half smile. "She does not know I am here."

"We will find her at once!" I stood, and he told me to be still with his finger to his lips. "What troop is Abrikita defending now?" I whispered.

"Yours."

"Mine? She's an elder. Why does she care if I win Prudence's girls?" Goosebumps energized me, head to toe.

"It is no trivial schoolgirl drama. She's fighting the pet hunters." Doron sat up. "I beg you to hurry. Get me in the tree and go home," his deep voice trailed. "Abrikita can only hold them back for a little while."

"What are they hunting?" I asked as a serendipitous feeling swarmed over me because my brother had spoken the same words when we'd played war. "Hurry. Go home. We can only hold them back for a little while."

"Listen." Doron pointed into the jungle. "A safari."

Shrieks and whistles warned across the tousled branches.

"Jackie! We're ready. Leave that old man alone and tell us what to do next." Kane hollered as Rowdy waved.

"Get over here, Rowdy. Pronto!" I yelled, and as he approached, I asked what Prudence was doing.

"Standing around." Rowdy bounced in place, ready.

"Prudence, you two follow Lilliana, and she'll show you where to get water," I yelled. No one stirred. "I will fight you and I will win. Do not challenge me." My brother's words erupted from my chest.

Lucella, who'd petted Doron, whispered that I'd made a mistake.

I stiffened.

"Your best man is on a stretcher. Really, who could you call to fight me?" Prudence called out with a bellowing laugh.

"Me!" Lilliana screeched and beat her fists in the dirt.

Doron waved for me, and I looked over my shoulder to see if Lilliana had blistered Prudence's nose yet and when it was clear Lilliana had it under control and was leading them to water, I went to him. "We'll get you up there. Don't worry." I told Rowdy to use his shirt as a wrap to secure the elder onto his back. "Lil is bringing you some water, and we'll get some fruit for you before we go."

Doron's head rose higher. "There is no time. Listen, my little Clementines."

Breaking branches, machetes' slicing vines, whooping men and barking hounds threatened.

"No," I breathed. "The pet hunters." My heart thumped against my ribs.

Rowdy grabbed the elder and Lucella secured him against Rowdy's back, and the young lemur pounced up against the kily trunk. His grip slipped, bark shreds fell over us, and we watched helplessly as he dug in his nails. "I got it," he said and pounced up the tree into the high branches.

Lilliana returned, holding two bamboo sections, and I pointed up the tree, grabbing one bamboo before she leaped upwards.

"Stay with them. There's no time to waste now. You'll be safe, and Doron will need you to lean on." I bit open a grapefruit from the jungle floor. "Where's Prudence and Catrina?" I asked Lil.

"I turned around and they were gone. Black magic done ripped them out of this jungle or they cleared a tree without a trace. I don't know," she said.

"I hope they're okay. I guess water was too much work for them." I handed her a grapefruit. "This'll confuse the hounds." I peeled off chunks and scattered it at the base of the tree, like I'd seen Harold pretend to do at Trumpet Creepers to confuse the fox hunting hounds, and Lilliana finished the job as I jumped off into the jungle to give the water to Brock. He was halfway conscious.

"Tell Mom I love her." Brock's eyes rolled shut.

A growling hound sped through the bush.

I ripped the bamboo section's lip, forging a sharp edge. "Run, Kane, and you boys keep up." There were six of us, including Kane, who carried Brock on the stretcher. Shanelle led them, a long stick in her jaws.

Without work, Neo looked around, and I told him to follow the boys. "See if you can outrun them, Neo. I know you can do it!" Again, Harold's words echoed in my chest. Neo's nubbed tail stretched out straight behind him as his elbows flashed in his dogged race.

Prudence and Catrina were out of sight. I looked up at the trees, through the jungle's kaleidoscope of shadows, and there was no sign of them.

I ran behind the troop, the sharp bamboo firm between my teeth. I held a grapefruit in my fist and stopped every few yards to peel off a chunk and tossed it over our tracks.

A growling hound's tail flagged white in the sea of green.

I spied a grapefruit grove of about five and yelled, "Up! Now. Throw him on your back. Up the grapefruit trees! The hounds are here!"

"Those trees are too short. They'll shoot us!" Kane hollered.

"From the grapefruit to the rosewoods to the baobab. We can do this!" I commanded.

My troop pounced up the trees, but Kane and the boys struggled with the stretcher. Kane had the head of the stretcher in his jaws and the others grabbed at it when it precariously dangled, but Brock grabbed the frame in a mighty save.

Maybe I was asking too much.

Twenty feet away, three tall terrier hounds targeted me. I jumped up and down. "Eek! Eek!" The bamboo carved into my knife jabbed in the air. I leaped onto the nearest branch and back down, teasing the hounds to try me.

The tallest terrier lunged for me and jerked my dress right off. He tossed it away and came at my leg, and I pounced onto a tree trunk, swung onto a branch, and shrieked over him. Naked. Powerful. Unafraid. No, I was afraid, but I was too something to stop. Was I doing this to secure my leadership? Was I doing this to save my friends? I don't know. I just did what I had to do. The other two hounds climbed up the terrier's back, one over the other. They were at my heels, snapping and snarling, when a loud pack of powerful hounds burst through the jungle bush into the grove. In seconds, the cleared grove floor was a sea of barking brown and white. Hunters hollered in the distance. "Sic! Sic!"

I jabbed the bamboo into the snapping snout at my foot and then another snout, and another. I jabbed, shrieked, and jabbed, jumping up and down on the branch. I was a wild animal. Wild and vicious. Grapefruits fell, and I jerked off the fruits, banging the hounds' backs. Fear was not in my vocabulary.

"Yip-rrr! Yip-rrr! Yip-rrr!" Screamed a ring-tailed lemur. I couldn't tell which one at first. But when his nubby tail swept through the trees as he made his way toward me, I knew it was Neo.

"Eek!" I warned him. "Eek! Eek! Eek!"

Still, Neo came. He landed above me and snatched a limb, chewed the end, twirling it in his teeth until the end was sharp.

"What's that for?" I asked.

"It's an arrow." He mimed, jabbing the arrow like I'd used the bamboo.

It was a novel idea. We'd only used bamboo all these years.

He pushed the arrow into my hand, snatched another branch and twirled it, and I jabbed another hound. He twirled another, and another, and another, as I jabbed one, two, four hounds.

"Yelp!"

"Yip, yip, yip!"

"Grrr-l, yip!"

The pack turned on the wounded, ripping them to shreds, giving us time.

Kane shrieked, and Shanelle waved from the top of a redwood, with Brock between them. Savages, we cackled from the magnificent baobab.

With seven grapefruit trees between us and the first redwood, Neo and I raced over the branches straight above to safety in the sky.

Redwoods are much taller than grapefruit trees. We each had a single arrow trapped in our jaws and took them out in unison. We toasted one another on the escape, holding them ready above the safari. Darkness filled the sunlit gaps between trees, and I shivered in fright, and Neo and I slowly huddled together.

We whispered at length about our families, and I asked him, when he was looking into my eyes, about his nubbed tail.

"My dad told me they don't know. I was adopted young. Believe it's best not to know. I came with a bandage, though, so it was fresh." Neo squirmed.

"I was adopted, too. We're lucky that way. Troops formed by orphans don't last long. They seem to fight continually for survival and end up alone and unprotected. It's strange." The world swallowed us in a realm, stranger than fiction in the dark shadows as day noises evolved into creepy night sounds and each grinding squeak sounded like a creature sharpening its teeth.

"Jackie, if we'd been in our own little troop, I believe we'd a been just fine, maybe more." He groomed my back. "You should get a nap in. I'll stay on watch."

I yawned and let my aching body rest. I couldn't fight it. Scared or not, my body shut down. I fell asleep and awoke in his arms.

"You were talking in your sleep." He smiled.

"I've heard I do that. Did anything happen?" I stiffened, and it made my body jerk. Embarrassed, I curled up into a ball but still jerked. I couldn't stop.

"Are you okay?" Neo tightened his grip, eyeballs bulging, and forced me out straight, working his legs around mine in a serpentine. "You're seizing, Jackie."

My tongue did something weird in the back of my throat, like it had its own master, and decided to overcome me and take possession of my body by choking me to death.

Neo pulled down a limb and forced it into my chattering mouth.

Sweat slicked down my hair and stung my eyes as I relaxed in his strong arms.

"Be still."

His nostrils flared as he watched over me, a grip so tight his heartbeat thumped in his thick thumbs into my flesh. Neo's lighthouse watch swept from me to the forest below and beyond, rotating from his shoulders. My fur tickled over my scalp, down my arms where he cradled me. The jungle's ever present petrichor filled my lungs with freshly washed earth scents in rhythm with the hissing cockroaches expelling air from their spiracles. Hiss-ss. Hiss-ss. The rattlesnake hissing sang a lullaby.

"Hungry?" He plucked a cockroach from a nearby limb and suspended it over my mouth.

Neo parked the cockroach on my tongue, and I drove the thick, vibrating bug down my throat. He ate a couple and fed me a couple more as I reclined in his arms, and I liked it.

"So, I uh, hope I didn't say something ridiculous." I worried I'd said something about his soft, dreamy ears. "What did I talk about?"

"Electric cars."

"I did? I read an article about them a year ago. I wonder what triggered that?" I sat up, stretched, and searched the forest floor, and the low grumbling growl of feeding hounds reminded me of my predicament—life or death, and my back stiffened.

"With electrical cars being all the rage now, the nickel mining company was on twenty-four-hour shifts, and they use 20,000 gallons of water a minute. Worse than that, they get most of that water from groundwater," Neo announced.

"I read about that in biology when we were using the class computers for essays on population growth, and I stumbled upon an article about electric car batteries and their contributions to the environment. None of their contributions, except saving money at the gas pump and lowering emission rates causing global warming, were good," I said.

"Yep. You failed to sign out. I read that same article."

"You're following me around?" I smiled.

"One bad thing, the electric car article didn't talk about was using the groundwater. The groundwater holds weight, like for buildings and highways, but when the water is routed away from its underground home, there's a cave left, and the weight above crumbles the cave. And it is worse in flood zones, like wetlands and along coastlines. There are megalopolises around the world, like Africa's, Abidjan, on the Ivory Coast, and everyone knows about Venice, Italy, and California's, San Joaquin Valley, and Indonesia is building a new capital because its capital, Jakarta, is already flooded. Mexico City is sinking the fastest and poor Magikaspar Island can't even get the scientists to visit. I believe it's the nickel industry though. The eight-billion-dollar industry is owned by Siberian tigers in a country with no primates, which explains why they don't care about what they do to us." He pulled at the tiny vegetation clinging to my arm.

My head was all swimmy, like Neo had been paddling around in my brain, and I liked that, too. "Thank you, Neo. I wish we'd talked about this earlier. There was a protest last summer. We could've gone together." His appeal quotient doubled.

"The nickel mine is on our largest seaport with 27,000 people in Traicao. It doesn't sound like much, but when you think about the company being the island's largest employer, with over ten thousand employees, it's humongous. The company bought the land cheap from lemurs who didn't know the value of their land and then brought in foreigners as employees," Neo said.

"Yeah, but locals won't work there or everyone and his brother will shun them, and we've even ostracized them from our troops. I mean, who wants to live next door to a two-faced lemur?"

When I was too loud, he held his finger to my lips. His own pursed up like I'd imagined they'd be in kiss mode.

"And those ten thousand employees wouldn't dare speak out against the dangers of mining along the coast, much less how much deadly waste is poured into the ocean," I said hushedly. "And don't even mention that the processing plant is inside the rainforest, less than two hundred miles from the city, where our endangered species try to survive. Wait." I flashed my black palms. "It used to be a rainforest. Now it's a wasteland. It's around four-thousand acres with over a hundred plants of concern, and almost seventy plants live only in that one area." Neo was engrossed. His eyes locked in mine. "Mom said her relatives, the sifakas, are on the brink of extinction because their food sources are tainted with pollutants. It's the same for my brother's relatives, the critically endangered babakoto indri. Harold has a short tail like you. But you'd like him because he's smart. Dad is a ringtail, like me, and our troops like the dry, hot desert like places. But the water contamination from the Ranomainty river near the nickel mine filters through underground water sources and makes our relatives sick, too." I licked my dry lips.

"This nickel mine is the largest in the world and is blamed for the loss of crops because the bees disappeared, for the loss of rice paddy fields, and for the deaths of adults and babies. Lemurs have increased birth deformities, more headaches, and respiratory problems. The company said it took measures to protect Ranomainty river, but occasionally, it still flows red with poisonous sulfur dioxide. The river flows through a valley, into streams and underground tributaries and back into rivers, down to the southern area where we ring-tailed lemurs try to survive." Neo wrapped his arm around my shoulder.

"It's like everything it touches is poisoned." I leaned against him until I felt his heartbeat drum. "It's like when the tectonic plates broke apart, and Magikaspar broke free from Africa and the war forced us lemurs to swim for our lives. And here we are, trapped again."

We sat in silence, our faces a half inch apart. I thought he'd kiss me.

Hunters, with their shining rifles reflecting the rising moonlight, warned us. Their tan suits marched around the grapefruit grove's cleared floor as they spat orders and disdain. Dark-skinned natives in brightly colored clothes carried shiny metal crates at the end of their safari. A hunter jerked a hound's mangled head from a pair of frenzied feeders, kicking one. "Explain this mess! What kind of hounds do this?"

Another hunter picked up one of our arrows, jabbing it upwards. "There's a man with them. The scientist hired a bodyguard. How clever. How stupid and clever do they think they are?" He threw the blood-smeared arrow into the treetops. "We always get our lemurs! Hear me? You cannot stop us!"

The moonlit scene played out in front of the troop.

The hunters, natives, and hounds pooled into the broken light. They peeked in and out of the moonlight as the kaleidoscope branches danced with the gentle wind. They drank water from their canteens and fired their rifles up at Kane and Shanelle while Brock's stretcher rocked on the tall branches.

It was at least eight o'clock when our bellies grumbled.

Double doors opened. A trolley sounded. A cool, sterile wind covered me, and the sensation of rising to the heavens pulled my hapless body. Ding. A door opened.

Sometime later, an open window curtain filtered the light streaming over my bed. White blankets covered my body. My parents and brother sat in chairs along the small room's sage green walls. A television purred out an old western and Mom wiped her nose with a handkerchief as a doctor entered, and my eyes slit open.

"Hello, doctor Abrikita," Mom's cottony blonde hair blurred past the end of my bed to meet the doctor.

She was short, dark, and intense. "Yes, good to see you, Lucy. I'm Surgeon Tay now, after many years of sacrifice, my new patients don't call me by my first name, but your family can. Jackie's growing up, a teenager. Have your hands full, Mother Lucy?"

Everything she said sounded like a song.

"She's a perfectionist and that in itself can work on a family."

"In the genes, I guess." The surgeon sucked in her bottom lip. "I went through that phase."

"We appreciate your honesty, your everything, expertise, and continued cooperation," Mom reached for her hands, and they hugged. "Did you stop her seizures? I can't stand seeing her do that again." Mom studied the surgeon's face.

"We believe the seizures are over, unless one presents from fever." Dr. Tay left Mom for my bedside and held the back of her bare hand over my forehead and quickly whisked over my hair. "You see, the initial labs showed a white blood count of 8000 with 91% neutrophils, thrombocytopenia, hypokalemia, and metabolic acidosis. She suffered severe leukocytosis. Jackie underwent laparoscopic surgery, and an inflamed intestinal loop along with an adjacent abscess were seen" Dr. Tay's prayerful hands clasped under her chin and fell and unclasped to her sides. "An abscess drainage and appendectomy were performed, since we were in the area, and it's one less thing for complications, and it was during this that we discovered her infection. The intestine had burst at least twenty-four hours prior, causing peritonitis. We cleaned her and applied internal antibiotics. She is a strong young lady. Now it's up to her."

"I don't understand. She didn't say anything about stomach pain," Mom said.

"She kind of did. She was taking up too much time in the bathroom. Remember. She had bathroom trouble, but she didn't talk about it," my brother said. "We didn't listen."

"She doesn't complain because her leukemia is in remission, and we were told she was good for another six months. If she feels bad, she keeps it to herself because she doesn't want us to make another appointment," Mom said.

"But she alright now, yeah? You spoil dat girl too much, cher." Dad clapped his hands at Mom.

"Better, Pat," the surgeon said. "She may need spoiling now and then and until we release, she will be spoiled exponentially. We ran her blood, and she's not in remission now, but not full-blown cancer either. It's developing again, but we caught it early." Her heavy words settled in a silent moment. "Let's be perfectly honest here. This interruption could impact her statistical five-year survival rate. She has a battle ahead. Her entire body will fight the infection while she fights the leukemia. Her bowels leaked, and we did our best. Now it's up to her.

5 THE AWAKENING

Kane and Shanelle pulled up branches around their bodies and Brock's for protection. It was all they could do with their patient to watch over. Brock's moaning made me feel better. At least he was alive.

Neo's expressionless face sent panic over my body. I didn't want him to faint, and his body language said he was going down. I pulled down a branch and stripped its spinach-like leaves and chewed them. Neo followed my lead. He noisily chewed while I groomed his back. I was on watch, and so was the purring threat.

Lord, tell me Neo will not follow me on this next move. Please. I gave Neo the hand signal to be still and grabbed some arrows. When I'd heard the deep purr, I scouted out the fossa and with my peripheral vision I found him just yards away, sights locked on us. We all knew the fossa was a hyena-lioness-like tree-climbing predator and loved lemurs. But this one was the one of legends, HUGE.

With arrows clenched between my teeth, I darted down the baobab onto a redwood below. "Eek! Eek!" I screamed, flapping my arms and the hounds stood up, about forty yards away, sniffing the air. I peered up at Neo. He sat statuesque as the fossa snarled at me. All seemed clear, with a branch above me, leading to a direct ladder-like climb to take fossa on a maze chase when a golden glimmer flicked—the fossa's tail. Fossa's tails flicked to signal ownership of a kill.

The mighty fossa stretched out over the two branches where it had laid and took a step toward Neo. He didn't flinch—that blasted, glorious autism.

The fossa lifted its front leg. It put it down. Lifted its back leg. Its paw rotated a full 180 degrees, keeping a firm grip on the narrow branch. It took a step forward. Outstretched his neck and tail, as long as its body, steady. He locked on Neo.

I was at least fifteen feet away, at least. I snapped off the branches above me to make way for a clear throw and the hounds spotted me. I jumped up into the redwood.

"Ruff! Ruff!"

"Yip, yip, yip!"

"Grrr!"

It was a clear shot, and the annoyed fossa snarled at me as the arrow bounced off his hard head and spiraled down and landed two branches below. Neo gripped a baobab's branch and arched back, ready with his arrow as I scrambled across the branches, the hounds livid with excitement. Bark and leaves flipped off and over their backs as they jumped up the trunk.

My arrow teetered on the far end of a branch where the branch tapered into a risky thread. I was four steps in when the tiny mouse lemur cooly scampered to the arrow. He snatched it with his teeth, and he lost his balance, but didn't fall. He sucked spit into his grin with the arrow between his teeth and tightrope walked toward me.

"Bless you!"

The mouse lemur stood on his hind legs, his hands talking as fast as he. "I heard you saved Doron."

A slew of mouse lemurs pounced and lurched from nearby redwoods, closer to us.

"Wow. Well, I have two good souls watching over Doron in a redwood above a grapefruit tree," I said. "We can only hope he'll be okay."

"You gave him water. We couldn't get enough to him. His spirits were so low, so low. Having his own kind help him made the difference, all the difference." The mouse lemur kissed his fingertips and blew them up to me. "You look just like his daughter, Abrikita, just like."

My eyes widened and slobber dribbled down my chin. But when fossa growled, I blew my new friend a quick kiss and rushed upwards with my last arrow.

Neo clacked, and I hummed back. Fossa was within striking distance of Neo's back. In sequence, we aimed at fossa and jabbed toward him with all our might. My arrow pierced his heavy coat at his belly, and Neo claimed fossa's fatal blow with a chest wound.

Fossa clung to the branch, panting. Blood dripped in long splats to the hounds below. Neo stood ready, a limb in his hand, twirling it in his teeth for another arrow. His concentration was the bomb. Fossa growled as his body weakened and his claws dug into the branch. In a slow sequence of steps, his head flipped down to his shoulder, limp. His body flipped downward, suspended by the claws. Fossa's corpse hung upside down from the baobab.

On the jungle floor, the hounds rushed around, yipping and snarling as the fossa's body slowly stopped swinging.

"Ka-boom! Boom!" The rifles fired and the fossa's flesh tore open and off. Neo jumped up to the next branch and over to the opposite side, tucking into a tight ball behind the hefty trunk. "Ka-boom! Boom!"

The hounds growled over the mangled fossa chunks. The men gave the hounds plenty of room, circling them under the fossa's four legs hanging from the branch as fleshy stubs.

Neo's tummy growled, and I told him to eat the baobab leaves. He'd been on watch for what seemed like an hour. The safari still swamped the shadowy jungle floor as hunters sicced hounds up trees for a scent of us ring-tailed lemurs.

"Does the pet trade know how ring tails end up for sale?" Neo shouted.

"I can't imagine that anyone would believe we would walk into one of those crates. Gracious! We're smarter than apes and gorillas," I hollered back.

Neo's palms flashed as he gave the what-now signal. He paced and chewed his fingertips, and I yelled for him to just walk over fossa's dangling limbs. I was in the perfect hiding spot up in the baobab and wanted his company. I wanted to talk to him. He knew so much. I craved his conversation as much as I craved Mom's cooking. I pulled down a handful of tender baobab leaves and stretched them out to him.

6 TECTONIC VIGILANCE

A bright light shined over my face as a set of sterile-isopropyl alcohol hands moved my bed pillow, and everything wore a strange pink haze as my body fell backward.

My flare began on Sunday, and we'd both been in our rooms all afternoon. Harold closed his bedroom door to finish reading Drums, Girls, and Dangerous Pie, and I knew why. He didn't want anyone to see him cry over the sad parts. Our parents were so lame, like a book about a sick kid could change anything.

My floor vibrated again. I was sick of it. My parents hammered on the clothes drying rack in the basement. I'd already told Dad that thing would not stay in the wooden railing because the moisture down there kept changing and the putty in the screw holes was like mud and they needed cement. I'd read it in an online search for "adhesives for damp places," but no, they use what's on hand because they're so cheap.

The distance between taps increased. "There," Dad said, "Now let's see how much weight it can hold." I was running out of time; my freedom hinged on my speed. "Crash" echoed from the basement. I made it to the kitchen door and had plenty of time to go outside.

I slowly turned the old chrome doorknob to the backyard and made it to my first jump but buckled to my knees when a cramp speared my belly. My body throbbed with the trampoline's bouncing waves as Harold's blockhead seesawed up and down. He passed by on his tiptoes, transfixed by the flapping blue flag he carried, ignoring me as I slowed to still stop and held my sides.

Ugh! How did he hear me? I was so careful, didn't even close the creaky back door. Taking a break from my geography project and there he was, uncombed hair sticking out every which way and peanut-butter-and-jelly smears across his tee—a real ape. I couldn't have jumped high enough to get away.

"No ball zone!" Harold roared from the ladder wedged against our privacy fence. He secured the blue flag on the snap hook and his stupid drone hummed over the greens as clubs whacked balls and players cursed the invasion.

We lived next door to Barkie's Golf Resort in Pinehurst, North Carolina. Golf balls sailed over the fence so much we kept a bucket for balls underneath. It was overflowing, like Harold's zeal as the overprotective brother.

"Look out, Jackie. Air mail!"

"Arff! Yip! Yip! Yip!" Piper darted under my trampoline.

"Ah, man, his tail." Harold crawled under and pulled him out by the collar. "That's it. Golf balls get up to four-thousand pounds of pressure." He tossed the golf ball toward the bucket and called out for Dad.

"They're in the basement and they'll be in there for breakfast if they don't give up and hire a handyman."

"We need to move your toys to the front yard." Harold held my badminton racket like a staff, up in the air.

"Toys? I don't have toys. Go back inside. I need my free time."

"You're the only one playing on the trampoline and swing set."

"It's equipment." I flexed my biceps.

"Swing sets have no physical strengthening capabilities."

I was sick of his dry speeches and know-it-all attitude. "It's for recovery." The last hurricane twisted the rusty swing set's ladder, and Dad tied it down with rachet straps. So, it wasn't a regular slide anymore. It was a slide stick and stop because of the warp. I'd slide my doll down, and she'd crash and burn in the warp. But a kid can push past the warp. There's just no speed in it unless you push yourself like a jackhammer, and I really didn't have the strength most days to bother. The swings were still good, though.

"These balls pack enough power to kill a kid." Expressionless as ever, Harold stood rigid. He looked like Dad with his dark Cajun skin and had Mom's blonde hair. I think that's why they favored him.

I thought about how unfair it all was. My baby bracelet reads, "Jackie No Last Name." It's in my jewelry box, turning yellow. Mom keeps a photo of me in the dining room's hutch. It's from the day they brought me home to live with them—a cream and brown sugar baby, she says, but that's all we know. They gave me their last name, Abbott, and I have the same blonde curly hair. But I am nothing, nothing like Harold.

"So, what are we gonna do?" I asked. "Put a roof up over the backyard or have you tote one around everywhere I go? You'd like that. Spy on me every minute. Huh?"

Harold held his chin and studied the roof slope of our brick ranch with his other hand.

I hurried down to Piper, and he buried his face in my hands. Our shepherd trembled and when I hugged him, I thought I'd hurl. Blood dotted over his multi-colored coat. Piper's German Shepherd whine cut through to my spine. "Dad! Dad!"

My entire family, Dad, Mom, Harold, and I, sat at the veterinarian's hospital while Piper had tail surgery, and they cut off the kinked end. I couldn't be still. My stomach churned green over the slimy drool hanging out of the nauseous coonhound's jowls on the other side of the waiting room. The poor thing howled every once in a while, but when the nurse opened the door, it wagged its tail. Piper ran straight to us, the leash dragging the tile, with his three-quarter wagger up in the air.

As soon as we got in the car, Dad called Miles Pargo, who he happened to know from his golf cart sales business. Pargo hit the ball that hit Piper, and Dad told him it could have been his daughter. Harold interrupted Dad and said I didn't have a tail, so I didn't factor into that conversation, and when Dad laughed, Harold did too, and then Mom. That's my life.

My problems are not even serious to them. I could've had my teeth knocked out or my jaw dislocated or worse, like my spine broken and need Harold to carry me around for the rest of my life. They didn't want to hear about that, though. That retired golf pro paid the vet bill. But instead of changing the golf boundaries, or moving somewhere else, like a place where I could have a horse or a pet llama or raise my own hammerhead shark in a tank and train it to fetch nails and tools and cool stuff like that for oil riggers in the ocean and sell it for a gazillion dollars, my parents decided I had to play somewhere else.

I had only one hope left. My parents controlled everything I did and if I won the summer camp tickets, they'd have to let me go and I'd be free. They'd see I could take care of myself and stop sending my brother to boss me around all the time. I was sick of it!

I had to play across the street at the four-thousand-acre equestrian reserve, Trumpet Creeper Acres. And we didn't care that the trails were covered in green horse biscuits because when the boys needed corralling, we had ready weapons. It was early May, and my girlfriends came over to play on Saturdays. We played war, cowgirls, and wild horse stampede, and marry me. It was the best, except my brother and his friends chased us all the time and threw their frisbees right at us. There was no way I could survive another summer of being the tattletale. Because it didn't matter when I ratted on Harold for breaking our stick horses and holding us hostage and not one of those boys would play marry me right.

They wouldn't slip one of our woven clover rings onto our married fingers and they wouldn't even say, "I do." They'd say stupid things: "Not you." "Fake out." "When you look like Holly Rivers, maybe." Holly Rivers was in our town for two weeks and performed for the school board and they invited honor students. Of course, my brother and his stupid friends were in love with her. My parents always said Harold deserved the role of a big brother like any other boy. I had to win those tickets. I saw his face everywhere I went.

Piper and I went straight to my room when we got home from sewing his tail. He laid on a pile of my dirty clothes while I completed my geography project. I hid my signature in the crook of Mississippi's tail end, Jackie Abbott. I glued the last additions, a tiny guitar and a magnolia blossom, and used tweezers on the tiniest additions. I'd acquired a bunch, like thirty tiny, barbed spines I pulled out of my brother's cactus when he was in the shower. I spread the glue into a cactus shape and placed them with the pointed ends poking out of the cactus' outline. I stood up and stretched and surveyed my state map. It was magnificent, all requirements met: the capital, waterways, demographics, and natural resources. "I'll finish seventh grade with the highest grades and win those summer camp tickets. I just know it." I rubbed my tired eyes, stretched my aching back, and fell into bed.

"Who to take to summer camp, Shanelle or Lilliana?"

I pulled out my diary from under my pillow and wrote the details. It was Sunday night, 10:15 p.m., and my state essay and map were due Monday. I loved geography so much I could marry it. Maybe I'll write a pro and con list on which of my best friends to take with me to summer camp. But it'll have to wait until tomorrow. My eyes throbbed.

Details, I thought. Like my map's extra details, I'd also added extras to my essay. I couldn't help myself. My essay developed into an induction into the way the world works. But we all know the reason I couldn't help myself. I was grounded, again, and I had nothing to do but read my new book on Madagascar's lemurs. Those mammals reminded me of people and war and how unfair life is, especially at my house. I have no say in my life, especially now. It's like they're all against me, not my diagnosis. Whatever I say just fades away like I never said anything at all. I'm so tired of it. That's why I had so much to say in my essay. My one-page essay grew into three pages.

I hid my diary under my pillow.

Lord, please let me win. I just have to get out of this house for a couple of weeks this summer or I'll end up reading the entire break and have nothing new to write about. I filled the past two diaries with nothing, but summers spent playing at Trumpet Creeper with Lilliana and Shanelle, and my bossy brother who always ruins everything. I must find a fresh adventure, or I'll cry all summer.

I ached all over by the time I tucked myself in and took a deep breath and must've sucked in too much air because I strained my belly muscles. I held my sides and concentrated on the world outside my window. It was black. The window screen rattled as the rain pummeled down the gutter spout and the sky lit up with silver strikes. "I hope that's not a sign for points taken off for complicating my essay."

I sunk in deeper, curled up into a ball, and worried about my chances of winning.

My nightlight's rotating cosmic stars floated across my ceiling, dabbing gold and silver stars over my walls, soothing my nerves. "This must be what the lemurs see from their bamboo forests—dancing kaleidoscopes of light and dark, only they have creatures moving about to make some weird shapes." I pulled the covers to my chin. "I wonder if they're scared of the dark, too?"

On the brink of sleep, the door burst open, and Harold threw a stuffed monkey on my big king-sized bed, and it landed on me. He hooted and slammed the door. "Nighty, night, dodo bird."

"You're crazy! You know that?" Harold always called me dodo bird, and it was so stupid because the dodo went extinct in the 1700s.

"Must be feeling better to yell from your gut like that." His knuckles knocked out a melody on the hallway's chair rail on his way to his room.

I grabbed the monkey and snarled. "Dad, he's bothering me again!" I threw the wet monkey at my door, and it squeaked against the wooden floor. It was Piper's toy and like all the shepherd's stuffed animals, it smelled like the fish oil we fed him to make his coat slick. He'd nibbled it with love bites until he'd covered the monkey in a slimy concoction of slobber and dog chow crumbs.

I jerked back the covers, hopped onto my pink-flowered rug at the side of my bed, pounded across the wooden floor, and stepped over the wet monkey, and doubled over in pain. It felt like a rope jerked tight around my waist, and it made me angrier. "Aren't you going to yell at him or something?" I turned on the hallway light and saw my brother's offering, his new book, Dragonfruit by Makiia Lucier. I tucked it under my arm and hurried to the bathroom. "He does whatever he wants, and I can't do anything!" I thought about the fish sticks and macaroni dinner and if ketchup can go rank.

"My peeshwank can't walk around alone!" Dad hollered. "You grounded 'til you learn to call us and say where you at. You got that?" Mom had banned Dad's Cajun spice, but the words blurted out in a symphonic masterpiece. "Gyrl."

"I tried calling and no one would answer their phone. It's not my fault you didn't know I changed my mind about the library. Like, I go to Shanelle's all the time."

Mom mumbled something.

"I can take care of myself. I'm thirteen and the fastest sprinter in my class!"

"You don't know anything, Jackie." Harold banged on his wall. "There's bad guys out there, bad, who are a lot faster than a wimpy thirteen-year-old girl."

I flicked on the bathroom light, and Piper met me in the hallway. His coat shined golden. "You're supposed to be in my room." I kissed the top of his pretty head and ached at the sight of his bandaged tail.

Piper slugged down the hallway to the bathroom and shrugged at my reflection in the dim light. My curly blonde hair was sticking out all over from the bed sheets static, framing the dark circles around my eyes. "I look like I'm in college, not seventh grade." I shivered under the air-conditioning vent and hurried back to my bed's cozy quilt and read enough of my brother's offering to find it uncanny he'd want me to read a story embracing women with voices that mattered. With a headful of questions to ask him at breakfast, I bookmarked the page and opened my brother's book that I'd borrowed from his bedroom last week when he was in karate class. His room was a smorgasbord of books, and I knew he wouldn't miss this one because it was under a stack of history books. For the Love of Lemurs: My Life in the Wilds of Madagascar by Patricia Chapple Wright was an adventure into another dimension. The lemurs had social classes and behaviors and food preferences and everything, just like us. I was on page fifty-seven when my eyes watered, thick with sleep.

I talked in my sleep. I knew because Harold mocked me. So, I was not only thinking about Mississippi and its one and a half million acres of federal lands, and if lemurs could survive there, I said it. And that's why Piper thought I was talking to him. Piper's stubbed tail popped against my tropical flowered quilt as he mouthed the stuffed monkey at the foot of my bed.

I rolled onto my back, and Piper rolled up next to my leg. I patted his back, and the cosmic night stars roamed over the shepherd's sleek coat as I told him it was his lucky night and that he could stay. "You need to be still, boy. You're injured. No scratching or you'll make my bed jerk around and wake me up. I have to get up early and practice my presentation. Deal?"

Piper licked my hand, and we closed our eyes under the floating cosmic stars.

In the morning, the May sun shone through the window across my tropical flowered quilt on the floor, an island of pink flowers. Half asleep and sweaty, I pushed Piper onto the quilt, and I spread out across my bed.

"Ya breakfast gettin' cold, cher," Dad harked from the hallway through my closed door.

My eyes slit open, but my thick lids won the war. And one of those weird dreams that feels real pulled me back into its realm.

I returned to the terror of tectonic plates scraping apart, and my bed earthquaked. Lightning ripped, and I gripped the mattress edge until my fingertips pulsed, fighting the ravaging avalanche of falling rocks. The ocean crashed on the shore, and my scalp tingled as I drifted further.

Piper's toenails clicked against the wooden floor as he scratched, propped up against the side of my bed. Outside, the rain pummeled and thunder boomed.

My limbs flapped around as I fought for my life against all kinds of primates, large, mean primates, with long fangs. I grew hotter and sweatier, listless. My mouth was a sandy, dry beach as I yelled for help.

7 MY FAVORITE APES

His monotone voice read a narrative connecting my dream quest with reality, saying Hanalei had joined forces with her childhood friend to save the Queen and right the wrong that plagued her, and in a remarkably timed blink, I opened my eyes as Harold's met mine.

"Hey, dodo bird." Harold laid his book on the table and cupped my hand in both of his and held it under his chin. A sliver of golden sunlight burned his brown hair blonde and cheeks orange. "There's nothing to fear now. You've mastered the jungle."

"How'd you know?" I pulled my hand from his grasp as I sat up on my elbows. I was in a real hospital room, with the antiseptic stink and beeping, and everything.

A smiling nurse hovered over me. Her nametag read, "RN Ricardo." Her cold hand patted my cheek. "He's been here every minute, Miss Jackie. He's told us all about how smart you are." She recorded my vital signs and said she'd call our parents with the good news.

It was real. All of it was real. I could smell it. Taste the dryness in my throat and my tongue's scratch against the roof of my mouth and see my hands and body in front of me and the glass room's curtains and the nurses' station and smell the musk of a nurse who'd worked on her feet all day standing with her arm over my head. I was wide awake, and when Harold stood up and kissed my forehead, my dry lips cracked because I smiled. The sunlight spread as Harold opened the curtain and spilled yellow over the table beside the opened door piled with cards and Harold's deeply set bookmark in Dragonfruit's pages told me he'd been advising me the whole time.

The nurse came at me with a syringe, and I told her to leave me alone. "I'm ready to go home." I swung my legs off the bed, and Harold told me to wait until the doctors released me.

"I'm hungry." I grabbed the bed's remote and sat up the head of the bed. "Is there a menu?"

The nurse said my parents were in the dining hall and would be right up and that being hungry was a good sign, and I told her that open occupancy was a better sign, and she laughed.

"Someone else can take this bed. I'm not sick." When I leaned back, I recoiled from the cold wires hanging off my head. "What's all this for?" Wires protruded from square tabs adhered to my scalp.

"We've conducted electroencephalogram tests to ensure your brain is functioning correctly and to warn of seizures. I need to run another now." The nurse held out the syringe and squirted clear gel into her palm. "It's not a needle."

"Ohh. Don't put that slug jelly on me." I squished my lips and held my throat. "I need some water." My curls stuck to the back of my head, and I asked for a brush and the nurse informed me they'd washed my hair.

"We all want your blonde curls. It's just like a baby doll's hair. We love it. And your throat is sore because you were tubed until yesterday," RN Ricardo said. "I need to run this test now because your doctor ordered it as soon as I told her you were awake. She's on her way."

"First, I need some water." I clamped my jaws and clamped my fist over the wires, threatening to jerk them loose.

"You can have ice until the doctor clears you for water. Okay?" my nurse said.

Harold took a step toward the nurse. "Go get her some ice."

And she did.

Harold reminded me that caring for someone meant making sure they were safe, and the nurse was only doing her job.

"I'm sorry," I told the nurse as she handed me the cup of ice. "Thank you for taking care of me, Nurse Ricardo."

Harold looked at me like I was a stranger and said Mom and Dad spent every spare moment with us and that I'd said some weird stuff when I was unconscious. "You dreamed you were a monkey. Guess it was all the wires and being picked up and put back down and the seizures. I wrapped you up a lot and sometimes had to hold you still."

"A lemur. I dreamed we were all lemurs. Wait. You held me?" I closed my eyes and tried to dial into the lemur dream and held up my finger for him to hush.

He kept talking about what all they'd done to me and my diagnosis and stuff I didn't want to know. I wanted to know the name of Doron's daughter because I was sure my subconscious had discovered my birth mother. I tried and tried and held my eyes down tight, but I'd lost the name.

When a lady in blue scrubs and a white coat entered and read the computer screen on the nurse's table, Harold identified her as my surgeon. A clasp held her curly blonde hair in a tidy bun behind her almond ears, holding her silver-rimmed glasses. She nodded at my parents as they hurried into my room. "Looking good, Pat. At least one more night to get her strength up."

Mom and Dad teared up and said God had answered their prayers and offered me milkshakes and fries and all the junk food I'm normally denied. I told them where to buy a pineapple and grapefruit milkshake, and they asked why I wanted that concoction.

"It's not like I want a clay and frog sandwich, cher." I giggled.

Dad said he was glad I was hungry, and he'd buy me a clay sandwich, too, but he insisted I add shrimp creole. "Ain't nobody sellin' no frogs to da chef." His belly rolled and laugh boomed.

The doctor's bright smile grabbed me. "My father's Cajun, too, remember?" she asked my mom. "He's a real raconteur. He even has a book now, One Hundred and One Folktales."

A short man with a notebook and glasses at the end of his red nose under his curly gray hair bobbed under the doorway and knocked. "Peeshwank smiles. Ah, my podna, little doctor Abrikita pulls miracles off her sleeves."

"Out of my sleeves, father." My surgeon kissed the colorful man's cheek and presented him to me. "This is Doron Tay, my father, and he's usually on the children's ward telling his wild stories."

I felt the color rush to my cheeks, and Harold squeezed my hand.

"I told him you like animal tales," Harold said. "He had mouse tales and jungle book stories and all sorts of details on what they like. Amazing stuff, really."

Fat tears splat over the white sheets, and my brother asked what was wrong. "Nothing. I'm sorry I've been so ungrateful and cranky and such a louse of a sister. I am."

"Oh, that's okay. I can be a lot to handle."

"So can she!" Dad said.

"My peeshwank, too; stay close to garder over her. Franche with nurses and I calme them down. My Abrikita and you will be good friends, peeshwank," Doron held a notebook to his chest. In scrawled ink, my name ran over the top edge, 'Jackie Tay Abbot. Animal stories. No boyfriend stories, per brother.'"

"You told him I can't hear boyfriend stories? That's not going to stop me."

Dr. Tay's eyes doubled. "Boys are so far from what we're conditioned to believe they are. Honestly, they're the crickets."

"The crickets?" I asked.

"Charm, kiss, and jump away." Her curls bounced and full lips parted into a bright smile.

Mom put her arm around Dr. Tay's shoulder and looked into her eyes. "It's time we were honest about a lot of things."

Dr. Tay's head darted to Dad, and he clapped at Mom.

"Jackie, we've never kept it a secret that you were adopted. But we failed you by keeping your mother a secret."

"You ain't gettin' her, no." Dad stomped and gritted his teeth, and with his arms spread wide, prepared to clap.

"No, Pat, not this time," Mom said.

The stifling scent and heat of four adults and a teenager in a bed for three days wafted out the door and Dad sat down while Abrikita told me the story of how she'd met a man her senior year of high school who she thought she'd marry, but left town and how she knew herself well enough to know she was too selfish to give up her educational goals and too smart not to.

"I've watched you from afar, Jackie." Her big eyes watered. "I feel like I've been flapping silent wings from one tree to the next to watch you on awards days and meet your mother to see the birthday party and Christmas pictures and have loved you so much it hurts. I hope you will be my friend."

CHARACTERS

Jackie Abbott is 13, smart, ring-tailed lemur. She becomes a leader of the class, aka troop of lemurs.

Harold Abbott is 17, is Jackies' brother and an autistic babakoto lemur.

Mr. Pat Abbott is Jackie's dad and a ring-tailed lemur.

Mrs. Lucy Abbott is Jackie's mom and is a silky sifaka lemur.

Zack Zootanna is the geography teacher, a gentle and old bamboo lemur with red hair and a bald spot.

Mr. Timetails is the history teacher and is a fork-marked dwarf lemur with pink hands and uses stilts to be taller than students.

Headmaster Intensity is an exceptional babakoto lemur at four-feet-tall, instead of the typical three.

Shanelle is a seventh-grade ring-tailed lemur friend of Jackie's.

Lilianna is a seventh-grade ring-tailed lemur friend of Jackie's.

Danita is a seventh-grade, red-backed lemur friend of Jackie's. (Prudence's girl.)

Catrina is a seventh-grade ring-tailed lemur friend of Jackie's. (Prudence's girl.)

Lucella is a seventh-grade ring-tailed lemur friend of Jackie's. (Halfway Prudence's girl.)

Prudence is a seventh-grade ring-tailed lemur friend of Jackie's who battles her for total leadership.

Brock is a seventh-grade ring-tailed lemur, and he is a typical obnoxious male.

Kane is a seventh-grade ring-tailed lemur, and he is a typical obnoxious male.

Rowdy is a seventh-grade ring-tailed lemur, and he is a typical obnoxious male.

Neo is an autistic hero and is a seventh-grade ring-tailed lemur with a half tail. And he is a typical obnoxious male, but a better critical thinker and is loyal.

Ms. June Gull is the English teacher, a bamboo lemur.

Mr. Timetails is the history teacher, a fork-marked dwarf lemur.

Doron is an elderly ring-tailed lemur on the jungle floor. He is a descendant of the queen of lemurs from Africa and plotted a war to save many species. In the end, he is revealed as a Cajun man who reads to children in the hospital.

Abrikita is Doron's daughter, and in the dream, she is the leader of a ring-tailed lemur gang, the Abrikita gang, who fights the illegal pet hunters. In reality, she is Dr. Abrikita Tay and the birth mother of Jackie Tay Abbot.

Book Summary and Chapter Summaries

When Jackie Tay Abbot, 13, battles a leukemia flare up and drifts into a dream state as a ring-tailed lemur, she is forced to make tough decisions because in Magikaspar, the females are the leaders.

Her story begins as she completes the school year's final assignment, a state essay project. She has been reading about Madagascar's lemurs and Mississippi at the same time. She develops a fever the night before the project is due and endures a nightmare that changes her attitude about her bossy brother and learns being adopted is not such a bad deal.

Jackie and her seventh-grade classmates dash up the towering baobab trees as pet hunters sic the hounds on her troop. Brock suffers a broken leg. Prudence and Catrina disappear. But Neo, the autistic boy, sticks around to help, and it's a good thing he does because Jackie is afraid of the dark. Will she overcome her fear when the time comes to fight for her troop, or will she hide in the baobab branches when the mighty fossa bares its fangs?

Exercise A: **Condense the above book summary into a one or two sentence synopsis.**

Chapter Summaries

Chapter One, All Aboard! Jackie slips in and out of consciousness as surgeons work to save her life from a ruptured appendix, although she is unaware that her leukemia flare caused the new medical problem. Her family works to treat her normally while she is in remission. In her dream state, Jackie kicks for her life on a makeshift raft as a fossa, a lion-like cat that hunts lemurs, swims after her and her lemur troop. She becomes a leader.

Chapter Two, Phantasmatic, exposes Jackie and her family as a mix of lemur species as she is dropped off at Magic Kaspar School, a ring-tailed-lemur-only school serving elementary through the eighth grade. Her brother, Harold, is a babakoto, which is a ring-tailed lemur slaughterer. She experiences lemur-only occurrences, reckons with being a lemur, and presents her geography project.

Chapter Three, Lunch of Champions, reveals the dining habits and status quo of the lemur troop. Jackie shows she cares for her friends and is an empathetic leader when her best friend is chosen to sing lead.

Chapter Four, The Magikaspar Nightmare, is action. Jackie takes to the trees as the leader and, despite her fear of the dark and suffering a seizure, brings her classmates to safety. Hunters seek the lemurs for the underground pet trade and the mighty fossa seeks lemurs for dinner. Through it all, she falls hard for Neo, who shares her environmental awareness concerns. He is the autistic lemur who shows them how to use arrows and helps save them.

Chapter Five, The Awakening, brings her full circle to realize she is a lot like her brother and that her birth mother "abandoned" her for a logical reason. Jackie learns the responsibility of being a leader when she stands alone on the forest floor and must kill the hungry fossa.

Chapter Six, Tectonic Vigilance, explains her family dynamics and events preceding her unconsciousness. Jackie Abbott's problem of being strictly supervised by her high-functioning autistic older brother. She wants to win summer camp tickets to escape him when she suffers a fever and dreams she is in Madagascar as the Island formed and is with a troop of lemurs trying to escape apes in a beastly war. While the problem with her brother is told, the silent problem of her mother's voice and her own not being actively heard is shown through story.

Chapter Seven, My Favorite Ape, answers connection questions. Jackie realizes love sometimes comes in the form of a bossy big brother, who has a lot of similarities to Neo, the ring-tailed lemur of her dreams. She learns her adoptive mother and birth mother are friends and that sometimes the strongest voices speak softly.

Exercise B: Use the above chapter summaries to write your own version of Magikaspar. Write anywhere from 2,000 to 6,000 words.

Exercise C: Literary Allusions

Directions: Provide quotes for each listing and expand on the book's significance in Magikaspar.

Chapter One

1.   For the Love of Lemurs: My Life in the Wilds of Madagascar by Patricia Chapple Wright provides the dream connection and matriarchal society angle.

2.   Dragonfruit by Makiia Lucier foreshadows island dynamics with fantasy characters and a matriarchal society.

Chapter Seven

3.   Drums, Girls, and Dangerous Pie by Jordan Sonnenblick reinforces family struggles with an ailing child and how a sibling is impacted.

4.   Dragonfruit by Makiia Lucier carries childhood friends on an adventure to right a wrong.

Exercise D: Find Context Clue Definitions for Vocabulary Words

1.   Discretion (chapter one)

2.   Phantasmatic (chapter one and two)

3.   Hairy-eared dwarf lemur (chapter two)

4.   Mesopotamia (chapter two)

5.   Mouse lemur (chapter three)

6.   Petrichor (chapter four)

7.   Megalopolises (chapter four)

8.   Sifakas (Begin with chapter two)

9.   Kily (chapter one and throughout)

10.   Quadrupedal (chapter one)

11.   Tectonic plates (chapter one and three)

12.   Babakotos lemurs (chapter one and beyond)

13.   Fork-marked lemur (chapter two)

14.   Bamboo lemur (chapter two)

15.   Lake Tsimanampetsotsa (chapter two)

16.   Crawdads (chapter two)

17.   Levee (chapter two)

18.   Antebrachial glands (chapter two)

19.   Reincarnation (chapter two)

20.   Hairy-eared dwarf lemur (chapter two)

21.   Weevil (chapter three)

22.   Dogged (chapter three)

23.   Predicament (chapter three)

24.   Quotient (chapter three)

25.   Disdain (chapter four)

26.   Statuesque (chapter five)

27.   Baobab (chapter three and beyond)

28.   Equestrian (chapter six)

29.   Mammals (chapter six)

30.   Kaleidoscope (chapter six)

31.   Electroencephalogram (chapter seven)

32.   Raconteur (chapter seven)

Exercise E: Discussion Questions

1.   Compare and contrast Abrikita the lemur and Abrikita the human. Discuss her importance in the story. Use quotes. (Begin at chapter four.)

2.   What is the state of cattle on Madagascar? (chapter three)

3.   Describe Prudence's and Catrina's attitudes. Discuss how their disappearance may be an allegory relating to Jackie. Could the author be alluding to Jackie's self-reflection and that through the humbling illness experiences her less attractive personality traits change? (Begin with chapter three.)

4.   How is Mom's lack of voice important to the story?

5.   Jackie wants different things as the story progresses. What are those things? Prove your ideas with a quote. How does her attainment and lack of attainment influence her growth as a character? What do you believe was Jackie's most important goal and why?

6.   What is the history of the French and Madagascar? (chapter three)

7.   Describe Lilliana's personality. Prove with quotes. (begin with

chapter two)

8.   Describe the fossa. Prove with quotes. (begin with chapter one)

9.   Doron has a significant role in the story. What does his character introduce and show about ring-tailed lemurs? (chapter four)

10.   What often happens to ring-tailed lemur troops formed by orphans? (chapter four)

11.   Discuss nickel mining in Madagascar. Prove with quotes. (Begin with chapter two.)

12.   While Prudence has four close female friends and wants to be the class leader, Jackie has two close female friends and is the class leader. What does it say about someone?

13.   Why was Jackie distrustful of adults and what personality trait did it enable? (Begin with chapter one.)

14.   Discuss the ring-tailed lemurs' diet. (Begin with chapter one.)

15.   Historically, how did the names of some countries and states attain names? (chapter two)

REFERENCES

Bolt, Laura, M. "Agonistic Vocalization Behaviour in the Male Ring-Tailed Lemur (Lemur catta)." Primates 62, 417–430 (2021), doi.10.1007/s10329-020-00878-3. Yip, cackle, and twitter vocalizations were consistently used during agonistic submissive interactions with both males and females, chutter vocalizations were used during aggressive agonistic interactions with males and submissive agonistic interactions with males and females, and plosive bark vocalizations were used across behavioural contexts but not particularly during agonism. Males of all ages employed all vocalizations, and while low-ranking males uttered yip calls at higher rates, males of all dominance ranks uttered cackle, twitter, chutter, and plosive bark vocalizations.

Learn, Joshua Rapp. "Why is Madagascar's wildlife so unique? Their ancestors may have rafted over." National Geographic, May 18, 2023, https://www.nationalgeographic.com/animals/article/madagascar-wildlife-lemurs-evolution-rafts.

Dockrill, Peter. "Scientists Find Even Lemurs And Slow Lorises Like Their Alcohol as Strong as Possible." Nature, 20 July, 2016, https://www.sciencealert.com/scientists-find-even-lemurs-and-slow-lorises-like-their-alcohol-as-strong-as-possible.

Opray, Max. "Nickel mining: the hidden environmental cost of electric cars." The Gaurdian. 24 Aug., 2017, https://www.theguardian.com/sustainable-business/2017/aug/24/nickel-mining-hidden-environmental-cost-electric-cars-batteries.

Dr Vahinala Raharinirina, Université de Versailles Saint Quentin. "Ambatovy Mining Project, Madagascar." Environmental Justice Atlas. 18 Aug. 2019, https://ejatlas.org/conflict/ambatovy-mining-project-madagascar

Connect for Water. "Madagascar - Rainwater Collection Changes Everything in the Poorest Country in the World." Nd, https://connectforwater.org/do/madagascar-rainwater-collection-changes-everything/

THE SOCIAL BEHAVIOR AND DYNAMICS OF OLD RING-TAILED LEMURS (LEMUR CATTA) AT THE DUKE LEMUR CENTER By Kathleen Marie McGuire, B.S., Georgia Institute of Technology, 2014, Thesis theSocialBehaviorAndDynamicsOfOldRingTailedLemursLemur.pdf

Lemur Conservation Network. "Ring-tailed lemur guide: where they live, what they eat, and why they're endangered." Discover Wildlife, BBC Wildlife magazine. 21 July, 2021, https://www.discoverwildlife.com/animal-facts/mammals/facts-about-ring-tailed-lemurs/ The most recognizable feature of the ring-tailed lemur is its black and white striped tail, which is about 60 cm long. Ring-tailed lemurs have glands on their wrists (called "antebrachial" glands) that secrete pheromones (a type of chemical signal) that they rub onto their tails and waift into the air. This is called "stink flirting.:

The Walk of the Two Lovers is in the public domain.

https://www.melodietreasury.com/translations/song99_Le%20promenoi r%20des%20deux%20amants.html.

About the Author

At home, Stephanie M. Sellers is a creative fiction writer and gardener. In her community, she is a journalist, and she is an English teacher at a community college. Visit her at stephsscribble (dot) blogspot (dot) com

Grandma Stephanie Sellers enjoys her grandchildren.

www.ingramcontent.com/pod-product-compliance
Lightning Source LLC
Chambersburg PA
CBHW081148170626
46809CB00010B/3131